Anonymous

Atlas of the Engravings to Illustrate and Practically Explain the Construction of Roofs of Iron

SALZWASSER
VERLAG

Anonymous

Atlas of the Engravings to Illustrate and Practically Explain the Construction of Roofs of Iron

Reprint of the original, first published in 1859.

1st Edition 2022 | ISBN: 978-3-37512-414-4

Verlag (Publisher): Salzwasser Verlag GmbH, Zeilweg 44, 60439 Frankfurt, Deutschland
Vertretungsberechtigt (Authorized to represent): E. Roepke, Zeilweg 44, 60439 Frankfurt, Deutschland
Druck (Print): Books on Demand GmbH, In de Tarpen 42, 22848 Norderstedt, Deutschland

ATLAS

OF THE

ENGRAVINGS

TO ILLUSTRATE AND PRACTICALLY EXPLAIN

THE

CONSTRUCTION

OF

ROOFS OF IRON,

INTENDED TO FURTHER ELUCIDATE THIS PARTICULAR MODE OF BUILDING
WITH IRON FOR PUBLIC EDIFICES.

FIFTEEN PLATES.

LONDON:
JOHN WEALE, 59, HIGH HOLBORN,
1859.

ROOFS OF IRON MATERIAL.

PLATE I.

ROOF OVER ENTREPÔT DES MARAIS, PARIS.

THE span of this roof would now hardly excite attention amongst architects or builders ; but in the year 1846 there were very few examples in existence of a similar degree of boldness, and the metallurgic arts at the period of the execution of this work, were also far from being as advanced as they are at the present day. The merit of this roof must, therefore, be judged by comparison with contemporary productions of the same description, and by reference to the peculiar conditions it fulfils.

The Entrepôt des Marais consisted originally of a large open court, surrounded by covered sheds, and by warehouses, into which the carts carrying goods in transit were run, for the purpose of examination by the Custom House authorities. After some time, it was found necessary to cover over this court ; but as the inclosure walls were very light, they were utterly unfit to resist the thrust (or even the weight) of any ordinary description of roof. The problem thus proposed to M. Flachat, the engineer of the Entrepôt, was how to cover the court with a roof of large span, and, at the same time, independent of the side walls ; and he solved it by carrying the purlins, rafters, &c., upon a series of built rigid girders, of a semi-elliptical shape, bolted down to solid masonry plinths. In 1846, large T irons were not rolled, so that M. Flachat was obliged to form the bottom web of his girders in two pieces bolted and wedged together, as shown on the drawing ; the upper web is simply a piece of flat iron, maintained in its position by a series of cross-braces, and flat clipping pieces ; and upon the back of this girder the structure supporting immediately the roofing surface is built. The purlins are of small T iron ; they are supported by arched bars in the middle of their bearing, which bars spring from the ribs in such manner as to resist any tendency in the roof to lateral motion. A network of rafters and lathes, of wrought-iron, is laid on these purlins, so as to divide the surface of the roof into squares of about 19¾ inches on the side ; and upon them is laid the galvanised iron roof. Each girder weighs about 8₁⁴₄₀ tons. The total cost of this roof per yard superficial of the covered area was £4 12s. 6d.

PLATE II.

ROOF OVER PASSENGER SHED, ROUEN RAILWAY, PARIS.

THIS is a very elegant wrought-iron roof, of a considerable span, and of a very simple and economical style of construction.

In this case the framing is contrived, by means of the various struts and ties, into a series of six partial triangles, whose actions neutralise one another (so as ultimately to resolve the effort exercised by the principal, into a mere vertical pressure), in a very simple and elegant manner ; and the dimensions of the various parts of the truss seem to have been rigorously calculated upon the rules laid down by General Morin, in the Third Part of the 4th Volume of his "*Leçons de Mécanique Pratique*," 8vo., Paris, 1853. The clear span of the Roof is 88 feet 6¾ inches, the height of the truss is 14 feet 6¾ inches ; and the tie between the subsidiary trusses is placed at about 3 feet 3 inches above the bearing points of the feet of the rafters. The latter are composed of double **T** irons, which are jointed over the struts, as it was not possible to obtain them in one length. The purlins, like the principal rafters, are in double **T** iron ; but so placed as to bring their upper surfaces flush with those of the principal rafters.

The trusses are spaced at intervals of about 6¼ feet in the clear ; and it may be worth while to call attention to the fact, that the boarding upon the purlins was laid in two thicknesses, of which the lower thickness was laid diagonally, in order to resist any lateral motion of the roof, and was fixed by some projecting frames, forming panels. The exposed surface of the roof was covered with corrugated iron. The cost of this roof, including the columns, was only about £2 per square yard. M. Flachat was the author of this roof.

PLATE III.

ROOF OVER PASSENGER SHED, WESTERN RAILWAY, PARIS.

THIS roof is another of the remarkable specimens of the constructive skill of M. Flachat, and it serves to characterise one of the decided steps in the progressive application of wrought-iron plates to the purposes of building. It is true that, previously to the erection of the Western Railway (of France) passenger shed, Mr. Turner had already executed a roof of considerably greater span than the one attempted in this case ; but the style of construction—the principle of framing—adopted by M. Flachat was so essentially different from the style or principle adopted in the Liverpool Station roof, that the student of carpentry may well pause to examine both of these works.

As will be seen from the engraving, the span of the Western Railway Station roof is equal to 131 feet, 2¼ inches, from centre to centre of the columns. The general outlines of the framing are designed upon the same system as those previously adopted by M. Flachat in the Rouen Station roof ; and the truss was made into a series of triangles, so arranged and so mutually destroying their respective actions, that the effort exercised upon the inclined faces of the rafters was finally transmitted to the columns, upon which the trusses rested, in a vertical direction. In this particular case (*i.e.* in the roof of the Western Railway) the principal difference observable from the Rouen roof consists in the substitution of plate iron, strengthened by angle irons at top or bottom, as was required, for the round rods, or the cast-iron struts used in the more ancient example ; but in reality the change seems to have hardly been called for, or to have been necessary, whilst unquestionably the greater apparent bulk of the plate-iron truss must always constitute a serious objection to the introduction of a similar system, so long as it is possible to execute roofs at all approaching the dimensions hitherto adopted, by the use of materials of the forms more commonly employed. Really, the only recommendation of these plate-iron trusses consists in their economy ; for notwithstanding the increased span of the Western Railway roof, it only cost £1 16s. per square yard ; or in fact, less than either of the roofs designed by M. Flachat, previously given.

The dimensions of the different parts of the trusses are marked with sufficient distinctness upon the drawings to dispense with the necessity for a description here ; it may, therefore, suffice to say that the thicknesses of the plates ranged from $\frac{3}{8}$ths, $\frac{7}{16}$ths, to $\frac{9}{16}$ths of an inch ; that the angle irons measured 2$\frac{3}{8}$ inches on the side ; and that the diameters of the rivets varied with the dimensions of the respective parts of the framing.   The strength of the various parts was rigorously calculated upon the same laws as had been applied in calculating the dimensions of the parts of the Rouen Railway roof.

The weight of the Western Railway roof, including the boarding, frames, corrugated iron covering, gutters, ventilating irons, but without including the columns, was about 125$\frac{1}{4}$ lb. per yard superficial. The strain supposed to be brought upon the trusses was estimated at the rate of about 91$\frac{1}{2}$ lb. per yard superficial, in addition to the weight of the roof itself.   As the Western Railway had been opened for traffic some time previously to the execution of this roof, some ingenuity was required in its erection whilst the ordinary movement of passenger traffic was being carried on ; this object was effected by raising the entire principals from a staging which covered the respective lines of rails.

It may be necessary to add, that the columns are prevented from moving laterally by the introduction of the cast-iron girders, represented in Fig. 2 ; from which also the lamp-irons, for lighting the shed, are suspended.   The architectural taste of these transverse girders, and especially the taste of their spandril filling, is of a very questionable character.

The comparative cost of the roof next to be described, leads to the inference that the system adopted by M. Flachat in the cases of the Rouen and of the Western Railway roofs, was needlessly expensive. In fact, the corrugated iron, or double boarding, is far more costly than any description of slating.

PLATES IV. V.

ROOF OVER STRASBOURG RAILWAY STATION, AT PARIS.

THIS roof is a curious illustration of the combination of the systems of converting the principal rafters into rigid beams, transmitting the effort they have to resist to their points of support, and of the resistance to the lateral displacement of the feet of those rafters by means of tie-rods and of intermediate framing. No doubt the reason for thus combining the two systems is to be found in the great height of the shed ; and in the objections the architect felt to exposing the lateral walls to the leverage of the trusses.   But the consequence of the mixture is to produce an unpleasant effect upon the educated eye, and to inspire doubts as to the stability of the structure ; which doubts, it may be added, will disappear when the details of the construction are examined,—even though the examination should not remove the unpleasant effect of the complication of the mode of construction.

The details of this roof are sufficiently explained by the drawings ; to which perhaps it may be desirable to add that the trusses, of 97 feet 5 inches clear span, rest upon the side walls of the shed at 50 feet from the rails.   The trusses are placed at equal distances from one another ; and there are 37 of them in the length of 500 feet nearly, covered by the shed.   The mode of covering adopted was to employ close boarding and common slates, and thus a very considerable economy over the roof constructed upon M. Flachat's system was obtained.   The cost of the ironwork of the Strasbourg Railway Station was about £1 10s. per yard superficial of the ground surface covered.

A very efficient ventilation is effected by means of the lantern indicated on the drawings : the details of this part of the construction merit particular attention on account of their æsthetic beauty.

PLATE VI.

ROOF OVER PASSENGER SHED OF THE GREAT STATION, AT LIVERPOOL.

AFTER considerable discussion, Mr. R. Turner, of Dublin, succeeded in inducing the Directors of the North Western Railway to allow him to erect a roof which, at the time of its execution, was unquestionably one of the boldest pieces of construction in existence. Roofs of timber of 100 feet span were then by no means rare ; but in ordinary practice that dimension was the extreme limit of span, and the proposition of Mr. Turner, to cover the whole of the Liverpool station with a roof of one span of from 152 to 153½ feet, was for a long time considered to be dangerous, and inadmissible. In fact, it was only after a series of practical experiments on some principals of the size of execution, that Mr. Locke, the consulting engineer to the Company, ventured to recommend the execution of Mr. Turner's design ; and even after the original series of experiments had proved the correctness of the system adopted by Mr. Turner, great hesitation seems to have prevailed amongst those charged with the responsibility of what was then felt to be so great an experiment. The roof of the Lime Street Station has, however, resisted every effort to which it has been exposed ; and it must always be regarded with interest, on the score of its having been the first attempt at the introduction of a style of construction subsequently developed to the wonderful extent observable in the roof over the Birmingham Station, to be noticed hereafter.

The following particulars of the Liverpool roof are extracted from a paper read by Mr. Turner at the Institution of Civil Engineers, February 19th, 1850 :—

" The area roofed over, in one span, extends from the *façade* in Lime-street, to the viaduct over which Hotham-street passes ; and from the inner face of the new offices, to about the middle of the old parcel office, on the opposite side ; the extreme length is 374 feet, and the breadth 153 feet 6 inches.

" The roof consists of a series of segmental principals, or girders, fixed at intervals of 21 feet 6 inches, from centre to centre ; these are supported, on one side, upon the walls of the offices, as far as they extend ; and from thence to the viaduct, a distance of 60 feet 4 inches, upon a box beam of wrought iron ; whilst, on the other side, they rest on cast-iron columns. The principals are trussed vertically, by a series of radiating struts, which are made to act upon them by straining the tie-rods and diagonal braces ; they are trussed laterally by purlins placed over the radiating struts, and intermediately between them ; as well as by diagonal bracing, extending from the bottom of the radiating struts to the top of the corresponding struts, in the adjoining principal. These diagonal braces are connected with linking plates, by a bar of the same scantling, and also with the purlins already referred to. The curved ribs are thus firmly drawn together and attached to one another, and a rigid framework is formed, upon which the covering of corrugated iron and glass is laid.

" Each principal, or girder, is composed of a wrought-iron deck beam, 9 inches in depth, with a plate 10 inches wide and ¼ of an inch thick, riveted on the top. The upper flange of the deck beam is 4¼ inches wide, and ½ inch thick ; the lower flange is 3 inches wide, and 1 inch thick ; the web is about ⅜ths of an inch thick. This curved rib is formed of seven pieces, connected with each other, at the points where the radiating struts are attached, by means of plates riveted on both sides ; these plates are 6 feet in length, 7 inches broad, and 7/16ths of an inch thick. The beam is also strengthened at the haunches, for a distance of 27 feet from the springing, by plates 7 inches broad, and ⅜ths of an inch thick, fastened together by rivets.

" There are six radiating struts in each rib, varying in length from 6 feet to 12 feet, the lengths increasing, of course, from the springing towards the centre. They are similar in section to the principals, but are only 7 inches in depth, being attached to them and to the tie-rods, by means of wrought-iron linking plates. This attachment is shown in Plate 10, from which it will be seen, that the top of the strut is made to touch the underside of the principal ; it is in this position clasped by the linking plates, and there secured by a bolt 1¼ inch in diameter.

" The tie-rods in each rib are composed of three lines of rods, between the two extreme radiating struts, and from these struts to the extremities of the principals, they are in two lines ; the sectional area is, however, in each case the same, being equal to 6½ square inches. The ends of the tie-rods, which are prepared with eyes to receive the bolts, are placed side by side between the linking plates attached to the struts, and a bolt is then passed through them ; it will, therefore, be evident, that if any elongation, or contraction takes place in the tie-rods, the struts are necessarily acted upon.

" The diagonal braces extend from the bottom of each strut, to the top of the one next towards the springing ; they hold the struts tight up against the principal, and, at the same time assist the tie-rods in their duty. These braces are formed of round iron, 1⅜ inch in diameter, secured at the top by a bolt passing through the linking plate, and at the bottom by wedges, instead of bolts, so as to afford the opportunity of tightening them up, should it be requisite.

" Each compartment of the principal is thus separately trussed and tied, and the whole is made fast at the extremities, by passing a stirrup iron, or strap, round the back of the metal chair, in which each end of the girder rests, and to which it is bolted at the side ; the jaws of this stirrup iron are attached to the extremities of the tie-rods by wedges.

" The ends of the principals are each fixed in a chair of cast-iron, resting on one side upon a metal pillar, and on the other upon the wall of the offices, or upon the box beam ; those upon the pillars are cast upon the upper cap, and those upon the wall and upon the box girder rest upon two rollers, which have the power of traversing a space of 3 inches, upon a metal plate, so as to admit of any expansion or contraction of the rib, though, up to the present time, no motion has been noticed.

" The purlins are each formed by a combination of three T irons, the centre T iron running straight from principal to principal, and those at the sides branching off at 5 feet from each end, so that they strut the girder in three points. The purlins are secured to the deck beam by L (or angle) plates, fixed on both sides, one limb being fixed to the blade of the purlin, and the other to the deck beam.

" In addition to the lateral trussing, which the ribs receive from these purlins, diagonal braces are fixed between each two corresponding struts, connected at the top with the purlins, and at the bottom with linking plates, by bars of their own scantling : thus the ribs are all braced and secured to one another, and a firm rigid mass of framing is formed to sustain the covering.

" The roof, as was before stated, is supported, on one side, partly by the offices, and partly by a wrought-iron box beam, which was constructed by Mr. Wm. Fairbairn, of Manchester. It is 63 feet 4 inches in length, 3 feet 2 inches in depth at the ends, and 2 feet 6 inches in depth in the centre, being arched on the underside to the extent of 8 inches. The upper chamber is 20 inches wide by 8 inches deep ; and the body is 13¾ inches wide, by 1 foot 10 inches in depth ; the bottom, which was 19⅜ inches in width, was formed of two rows of plates, ₁₆ths of an inch in thickness in the middle, and ₁₆ths of an inch at each end ; the thickness of all the other plates was ₁₆ths of an inch. On the opposite side, the roof is supported on seventeen cast-iron columns ; one under each rib, at intervals of 21 feet 6 inches apart, from centre to centre, and securely fastened into stones five tons in weight, about 3 feet below the base. These columns are of the Roman Doric order, each averaging nineteen feet in height from the base to the capital, and 4 feet 3 inches from the capital to the metal chair, in which the end of the principal rests ; this latter portion forms the abutment, or attachment piece, for the intermediate cast-iron arches, with ornamental spandrils.

" The gutters are of cast-iron, 1 foot 8 inches wide, resting upon the columns and the intermediate arches ; the upper part of the gutter is splayed to the rake of the roof, and to this the corrugated sheeting is fixed by galvanised bolts, 5 inches apart. The rain water is carried off, on one side by the columns, and on the other by pipes placed against the face of the wall.

"The roof is covered with galvanised, corrugated wrought-iron, and with rough plate glass. The corrugated iron is No. 16 wire gauge, in sheets averaging 7 feet 6 inches in length, by 2 feet 8 inches broad ; which are fastened together with galvanised rivets and washers. The glass is ⅜ths of an inch thick, in plates 12 feet 4 inches long, by 3 feet 6 inches wide ; these plates are bedded upon iron sash-bars, at the sides, and rest upon Z iron at the ends, the upper flange of which receives the glass, and the lower one the corrugated sheeting. This connection is made tight by lead flashing, which is turned under the glass, and over the corrugated sheeting. The cost of this roof was about £2 per superficial yard, and the time occupied in its erection was about ten months."

PLATE VII.

ROOF OVER PASSENGER SHED, OVER JOINT RAILWAY STATION, NEW STREET, BIRMINGHAM.

THE series of Plates immediately preceding the one now under consideration, strikingly illustrates the influence of the introduction of the railway system upon the development of the arts of construction ; and of the gradual manner in which the demand for the application of science to the ordinary purposes of life is becoming day by day more urgent. Even within the last ten years, roofs of above 100 feet in span were considered to be great engineering triumphs ; and the construction of the Liverpool roof was regarded as a hazardous experiment. No sooner, however, had Mr. Turner solved the problem of roofing great spans of about 150 feet, economically and satisfactorily, than Railway Engineers called upon their contractors to effect more extraordinary things still ; and, in the case immediately before us, they no longer hesitated to require the execution of a roof with the maximum clear span of 212 feet. Messrs. Fox and Henderson, assisted by Mr. E. A. Cowper, have successfully solved the difficulties of this case ; and they have erected the truly wonderful structure, the roof of which is represented in Plate No. 7. It would be impossible to describe this work in more suitable terms than those used by Mr. Cowper himself, in the notice upon the Birmingham roof, inserted in the Proceedings of the Institution of Mechanical Engineers for July 26th, 1854 ; and the following notice has therefore been extracted, by permission, from that publication :—

" This roof, which covers the New Street Station recently opened in Birmingham, is in one span, without intermediate supports, being considerably larger than any roof previously constructed ; and on this account the present description of the construction is laid before the Institution as a record, by the Author, by whom the original drawings and calculations were made for the contractors, Messrs. Fox, Henderson, and Co.

" Under the roof are ten parallel lines of railway, with four platforms, and a carriage road, extending the whole length of the roof, for the accommodation of the traffic of three railways, with trains to and from six different directions (London, Liverpool, Derby, Bristol, Dudley, and Walsall), and having 170 trains arriving or departing daily.

" The whole length of the roof is 864 feet, and it is constructed of 36 principals, fixed at 24 feet distance from each other.

"The span of the principals varies from 211 feet to 191 feet. The ground being irregular in plan, and the space valuable, the outline of the roof was made to follow its boundary, and the roof is constructed tapering in two different proportions. The lengths of the several principals are consequently all different, the greatest span being 211 feet at one end of the roof, and the span diminishing to 191 feet at the other end.

"All the principals are *similar*, each successive one from the largest being reduced proportionately in the length of every part, so that the lines in each portion converge to one point ; and, in consequence, the effect of the irregularity in outline is not perceptible under the roof, and is only observed on examining the outside, at the back.

"The roof is supported on one side upon brick pilasters, projecting from the wall of the office buildings, and on the other side upon hollow cast-iron columns, 2 feet diameter, and 5¼ tons weight each, which are connected together by cast-iron arched girders. The height of the springing of the principals is 33 feet above the level of the railway ; the rise of the tie-rod, which forms a curve, is 17 feet in the centre of the largest principal, and the depth of the curved principal is 23 feet, making the rise of the main rib 40 feet, and the total height is 84 feet to the top of the louvre in the centre of the roof.

"The main rib of each principal is shown in Plate 7, and consists of a vertical plate of wrought iron, 15 inches deep, and ⅝ths of an inch thick, with two angle-irons 6 by 3 inches, rivetted upon each edge, forming a flange at top and bottom 12¾ inches wide ; the junctions of the angle-irons are made to break joints with one another, and junction plates are rivetted on each side of the vertical rib, at the joinings.

"The tie-rod is 4 inches diameter, enlarged at the ends where screwed, so as to preserve the full sectional area at the bottom of the thread ; and the several portions of the tie-rod are joined at the foot of each strut by a wrought-iron coupling-box, with a right and left handed screw.

"There are in each principal 12 vertical struts, each constructed of four angle-irons set diagonally in the four angles of a square, and separated by series of small cast-iron crosses secured by bolts passing through the hollow arms of the cross ; these struts are enlarged in the middle, to give the requisite strength, by proportioning the length of the crosses, so as to give a curved outline. Each end of the strut is secured to a cast-iron shoe, the upper one being bolted to the bottom flange of the main rib, and the lower one clips the coupling-box of the tie-rod. The diagonals in the principals are of flat iron, ⅜ inch thick, and from 3 to 5 inches wide ; they are rivetted together where they cross, and attached at each end by bolts to lugs upon the cast-iron shoes.

"The foot of each principal on the wall side has a cast-iron bed-plate rivetted on the underside, which is recessed into a stone, built into the top of the pilaster. The foot of the principal at the column has a flat wrought-iron bed-plate, resting upon four wrought-iron rollers, 2 inches diameter, and 19 inches long, which work upon a corresponding cast-iron plate, fixed on the top of the column, to allow for the expansion and contraction of the principal, from variation in temperature.

"The purlins are fixed at 10 feet intervals, and consist each of a wood batten, 6 inches square, trussed with a ¾ inch iron rod ; the cast-iron shoe at each end clips the back of the principal, and it is bolted to it, serving as an abutment for the two adjoining purlins.

"A large louvre, for ventilation, 5 feet in height at the sides, is fixed along the whole length of the ridge. Diagonal wind-ties, 1¼ inch diameter, extend over the whole roof, starting from the foot of every alternate principal, and bolted to the main ribs at each intersection.

"One half of each side of the roof is glazed, and also the louvre in the centre, amounting to $\frac{7}{10}$ths of the surface ; the rest is covered with galvanised corrugated iron of the thickness of No. 18 wire gauge, which is nailed down upon wood purlins. The glass is rough-rolled fluted plate, from Messrs. Chance's works, $\frac{3}{16}$ths of an inch thick, or 44 oz. per foot, each plate being 6 feet long by 16 inches wide. The total area of glass is 94,000 square feet, weighing about 115 tons ; the whole area of the roof is 175,600 square feet, or rather more than 4 acres.

" The skylight is constructed in three portions on each side of the roof, each one being a plane about 17 feet wide, and the whole length of the roof, and at a less slope than the adjoining portion below, the least slope being 3 to 1 ; the corrugated iron between the skylight and the louvre is blocked up from the curved back of the principals at the upper portion, so as to form a uniform slope of 5 to 1.

" Each end of the roof is closed by a glazed screen down to the horizontal line of the springing. The erection of the roof was completed in May, 1854."

The total weight of iron work raised was 1050 tons, which was effected without any accident to the crowds of people daily passing through the station. The number of squares measured on the plan was 1705, and including 320 additional squares of ridge and furrow roofing, supported on bow-string trusses, and varying in span from 188 feet to 45 feet, the price was £1 8s. 9½d. per yard, or £32,274 ; but this price cannot be considered as a criterion now, the contract having been taken when iron was at an unprecedentedly low price. The last principal was completed in position on the anniversary of fixing the first column.

PLATE VIII.

DESIGN FOR AN IRON ROOF FOR SHIP-BUILDING, HAVING THREE CRANES.

THIS roof was designed of cast-iron, and constructed to sustain three cranes to facilitate the construction of the vessel on the slip, one gang of workmen being able to work on each side at the same time, and one in the interior of the hull. The curved form of the roof was intended to give it additional stiffness to resist storms. The longitudinal trussing of this roof is also a series of curved trusses. The side roof had also cranes.

DESIGN FOR AN IRON ROOF FOR SHIP-BUILDING, HAVING ONE CRANE.

THIS roof was designed to be 80 feet in one span, without tension bars, and also of the curved form, and constructed with one crane in the centre, and two in the side roofs. Every portion, except the standards, was constructed of cast-iron.

PLATE IX.

LONGITUDINAL SECTION AND FLANK ELEVATION OF DITTO, WITH SCALE.

PLATE X.

GENERAL PLAN, COVERED PLAN, CAST-IRON GUTTERS, CORRUGATED IRON PLATING, ROUGH PLATE GLASS LIGHT, CAST-IRON PLATING, CORRUGATED IRON PLATING, SIDE SHED, GROUND PLAN OF DITTO.

PLATES XI. XII. XIII. XIV. XV.

IRON ROOF FOR THEATRE, BUENOS AYRES.

THIS roof was designed to show the application of the lattice principle to roofs required to sustain great external pressure and suspend a loaded floor.

In this particular case the roof was expected to be frequently subject to heavy gales of wind at a high velocity, and to be capable of sustaining a promenade for visitors in summer, to support the drop-scenes and working machinery for the stage, and also a general store-room, carpenters' and painters' workshops.

These five drawings will fully explain the character and details of the design.

This roof was entirely constructed of wrought-iron, except the gutters and ornamental portions of the balustrade, &c.

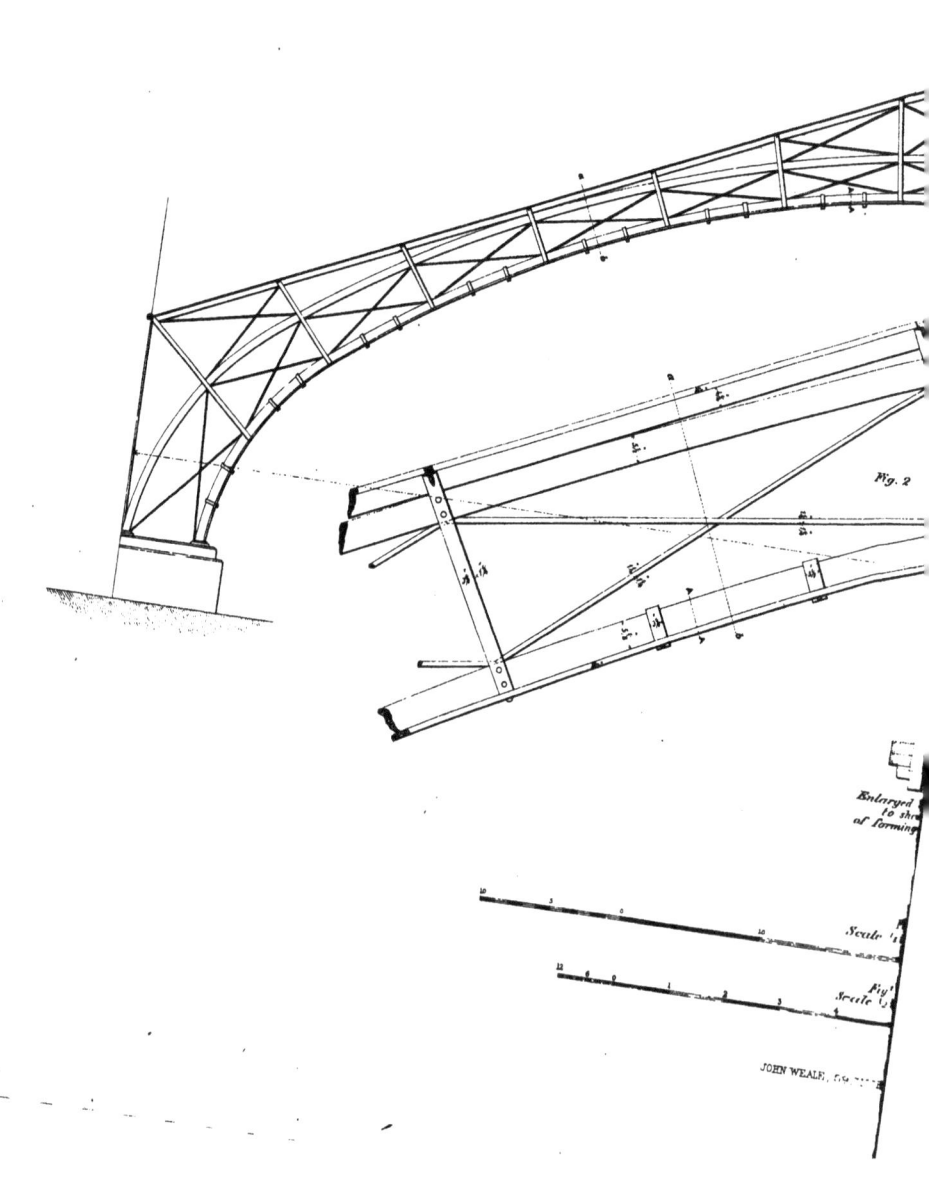

Fig. 2

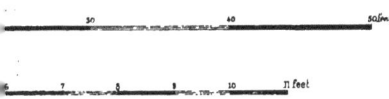

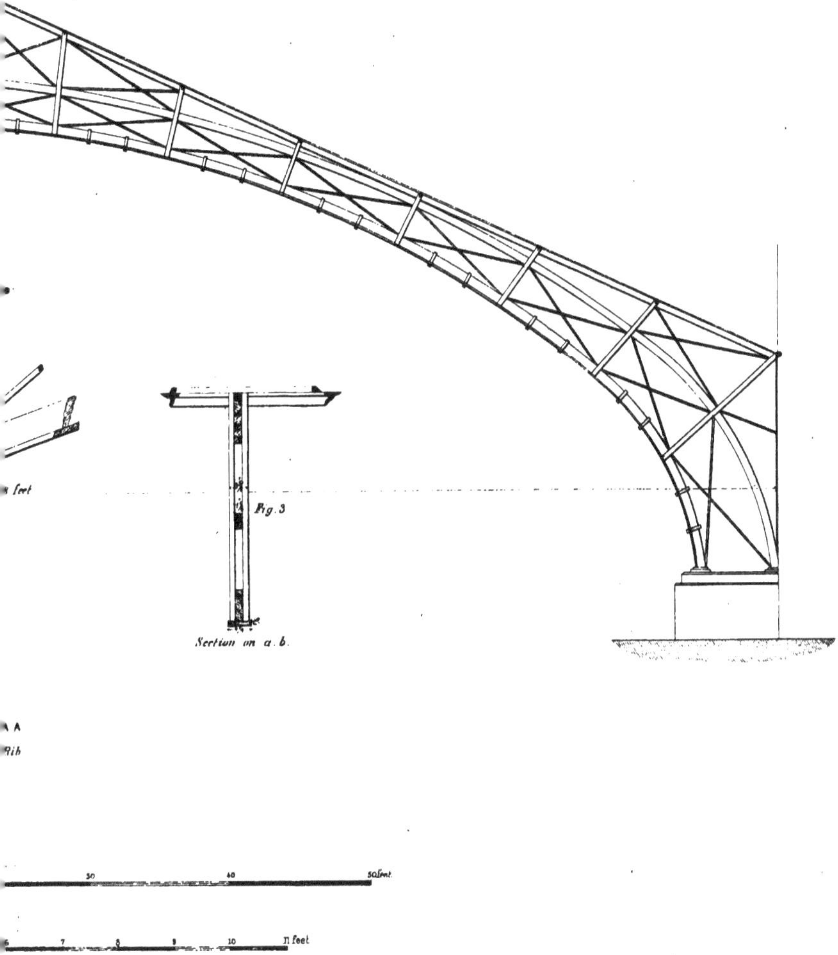

feet
Fig. 3
Section on a. b.
A
Rib
30
40
50 feet
6
7
8
9
10
11 feet

ARCH 1859.

KELL BROS, LITHRS CASTLE ST, HOLBORN.

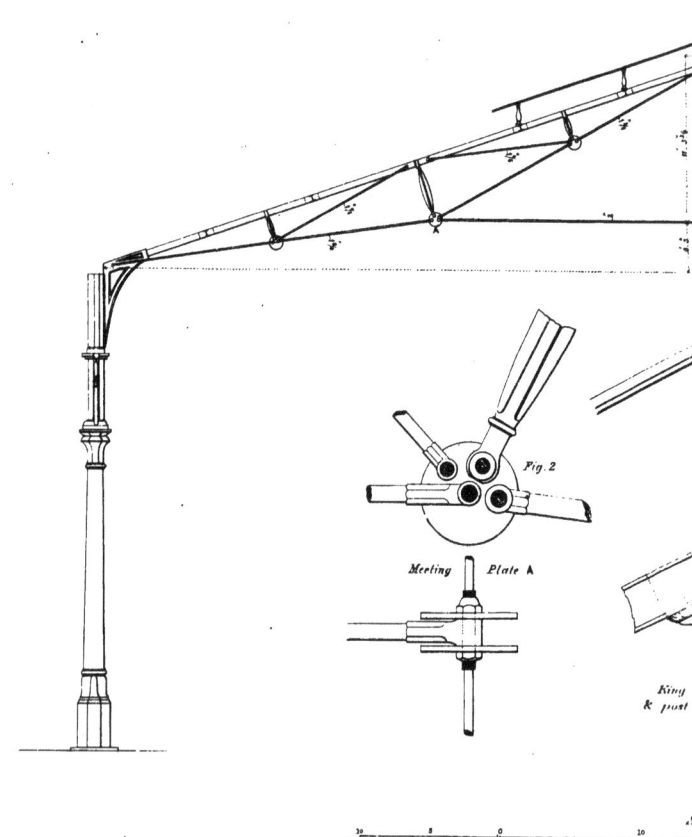

Fig. 2

Meeting Plate A

King
k post

Scale

inch'13

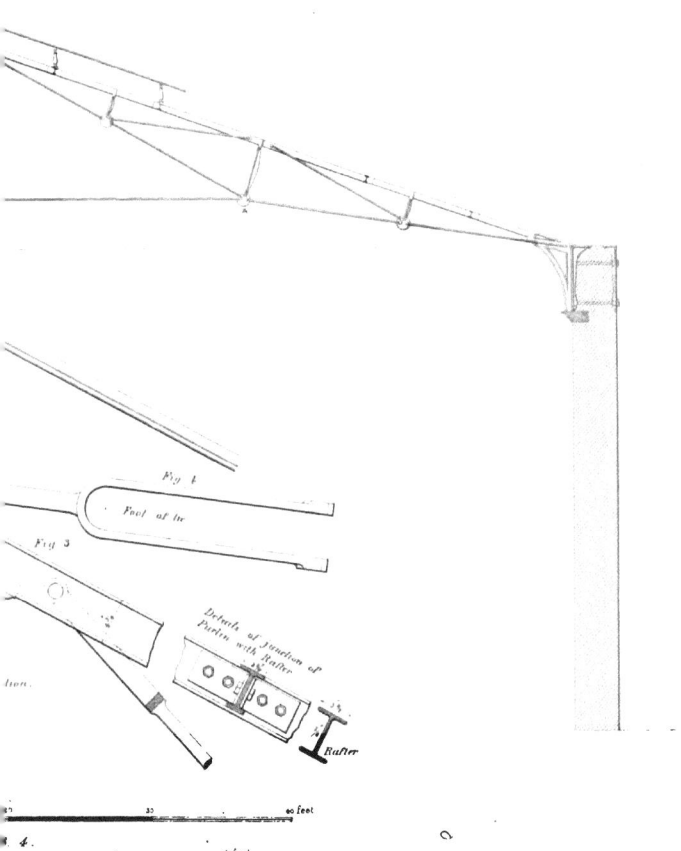

Fig 4

Foot of tie

Fig 3

Details of Junction of
Purlin with Rafter

I Rafter

tion.

40 feet

4.

4 feet

.

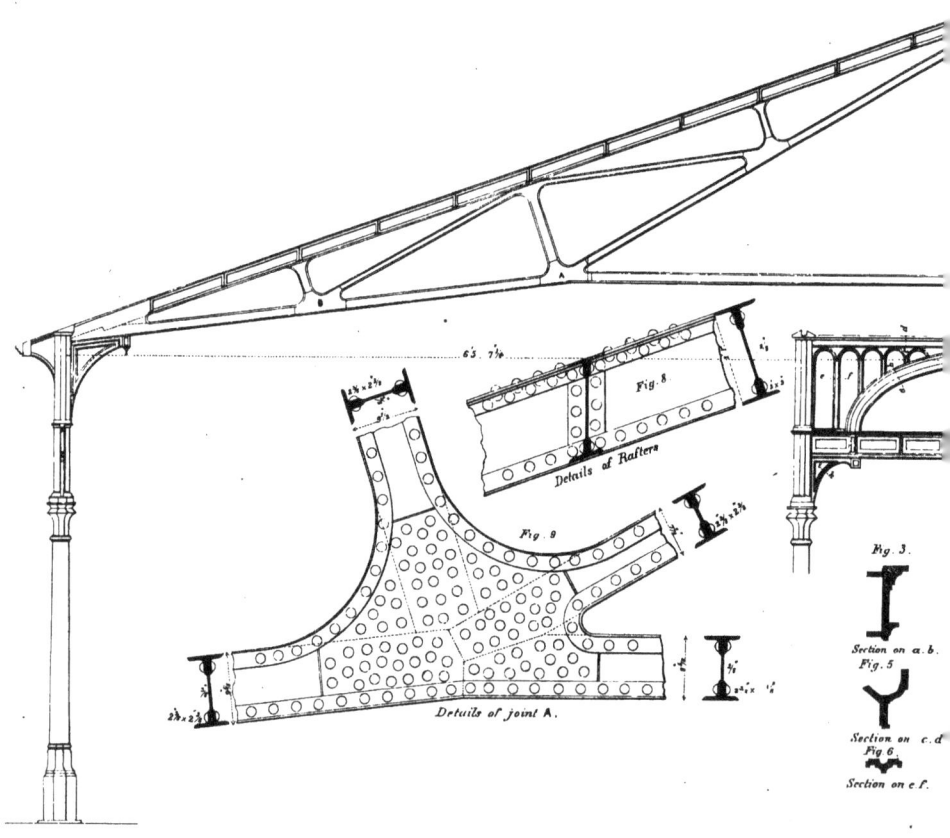

6's. 7½

Fig. 8.

Details of Rafters

Fig. 9

Details of joint A.

Fig. 3.

Section on a.b.
Fig. 5

Section on c.d
Fig 6

Section on e.f.

Scale

Scale for P

inch⁵ 12

JOHN WEALE, 59.

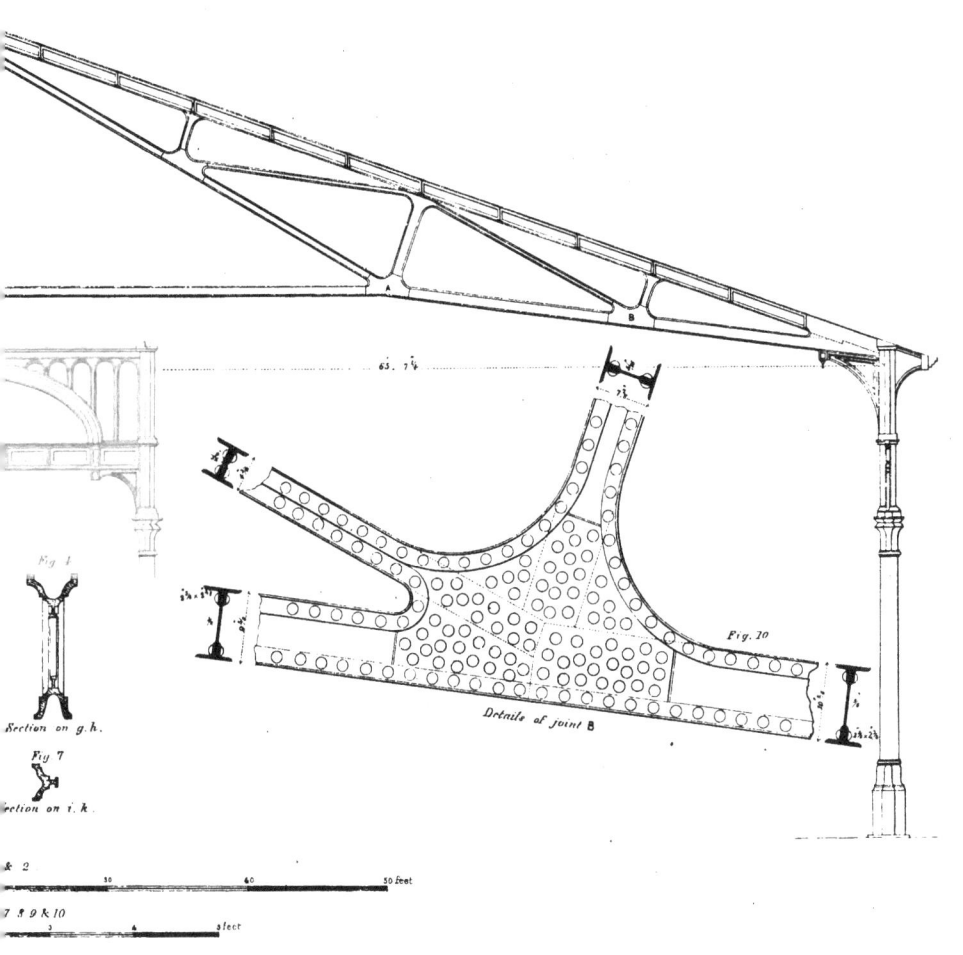

Fig. 4

Fig. 10

Section on g. h.

Fig 7

Section on i. k.

Details of Joint B

63. 7¼

50 feet

5 feet

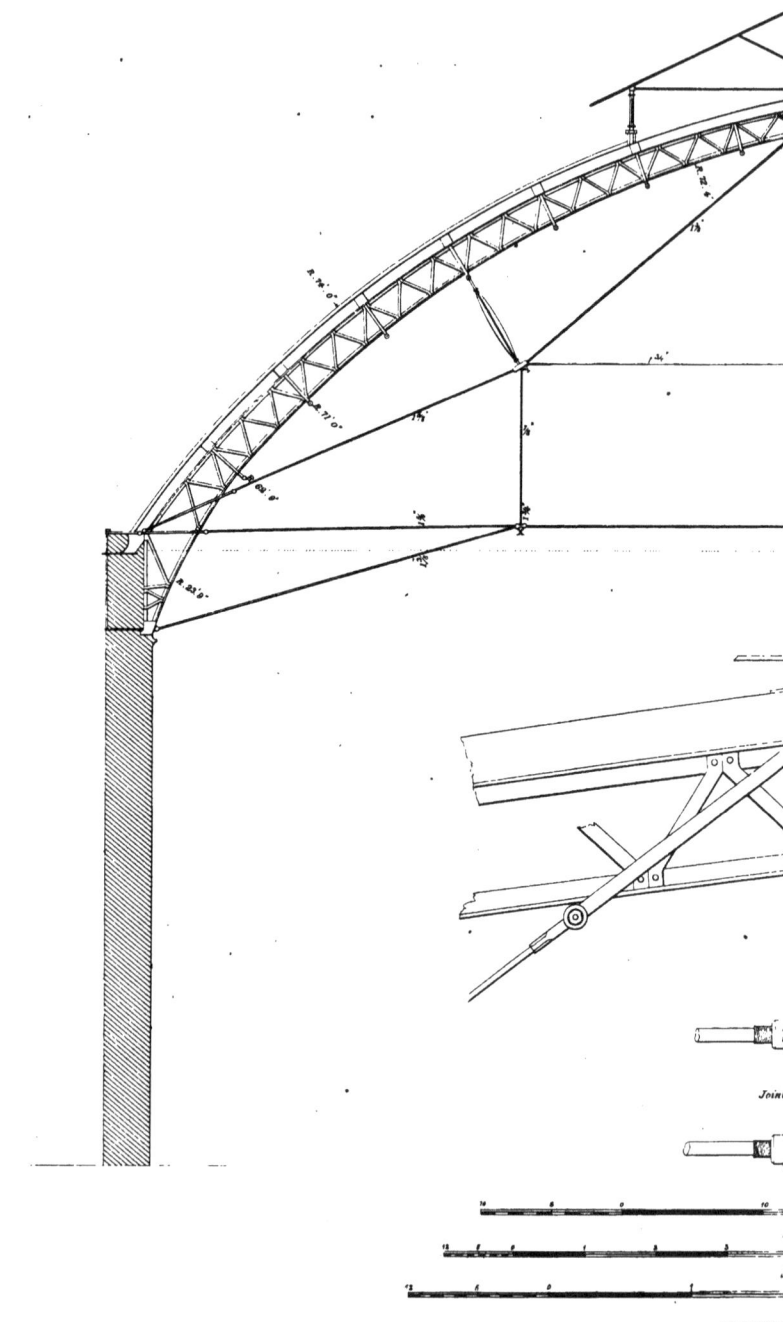

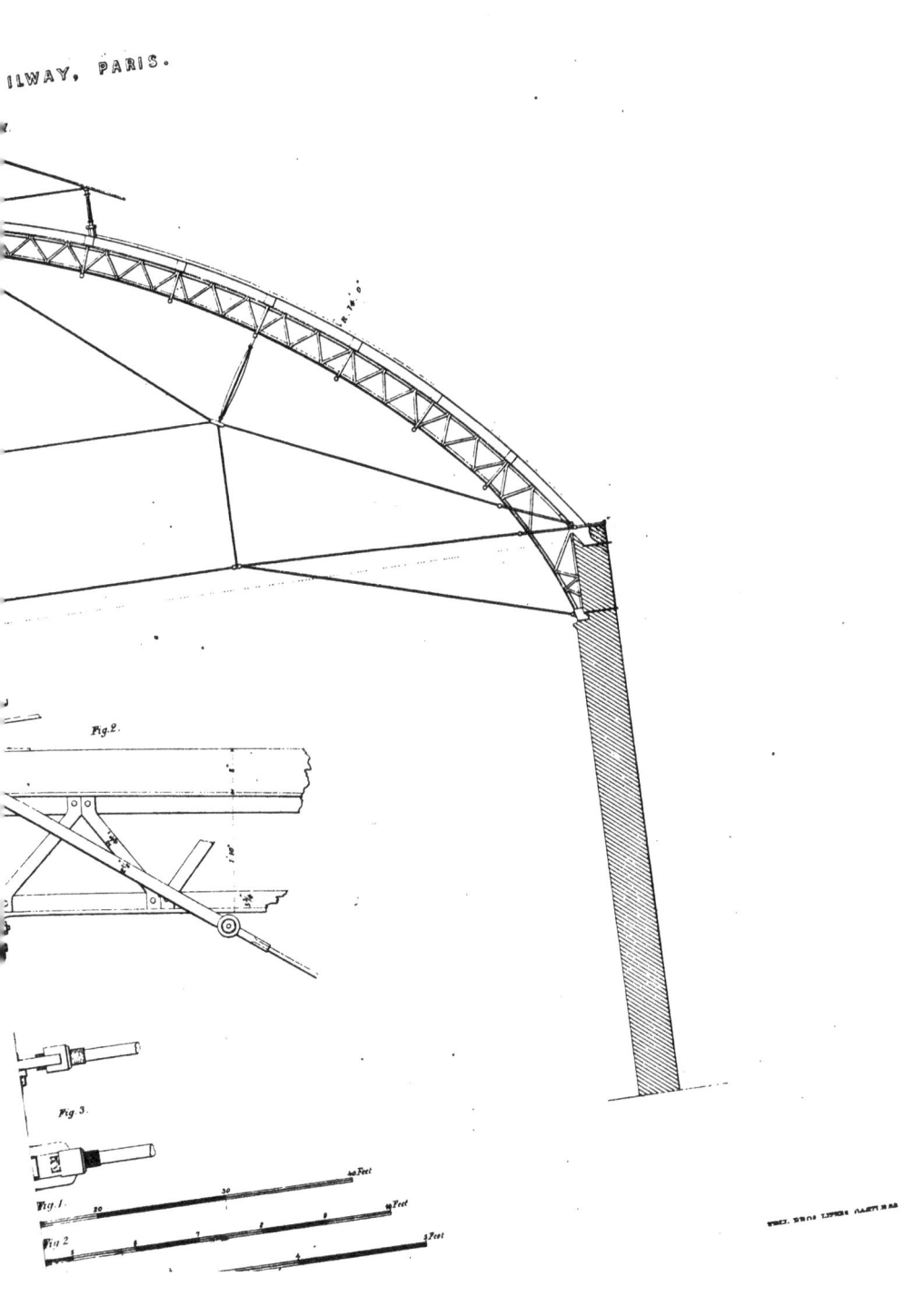

Fig.2.

Fig.3.

Fig.1.

Fig.2

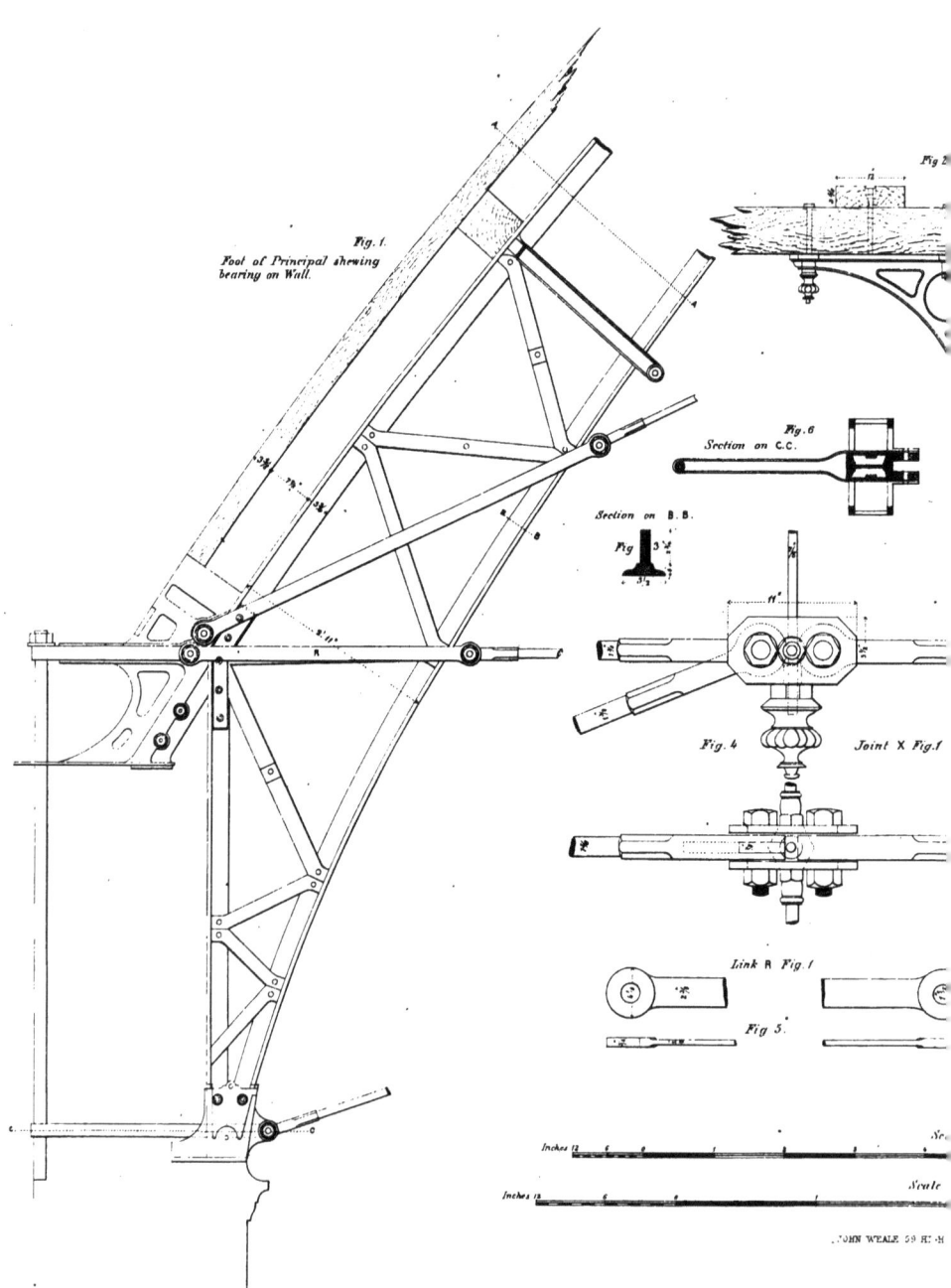

Fig. 1.

Foot of Principal shewing
bearing on Wall.

Fig. 2

Fig. 6
Section on C.C.

Section on B.B.

Fig. 3

Fig. 4

Joint X Fig. 1

R

Link R Fig. 1

Fig. 5.

Inches 12

Scale

Inches 12

Scale

JOHN WEALE 59 H! H

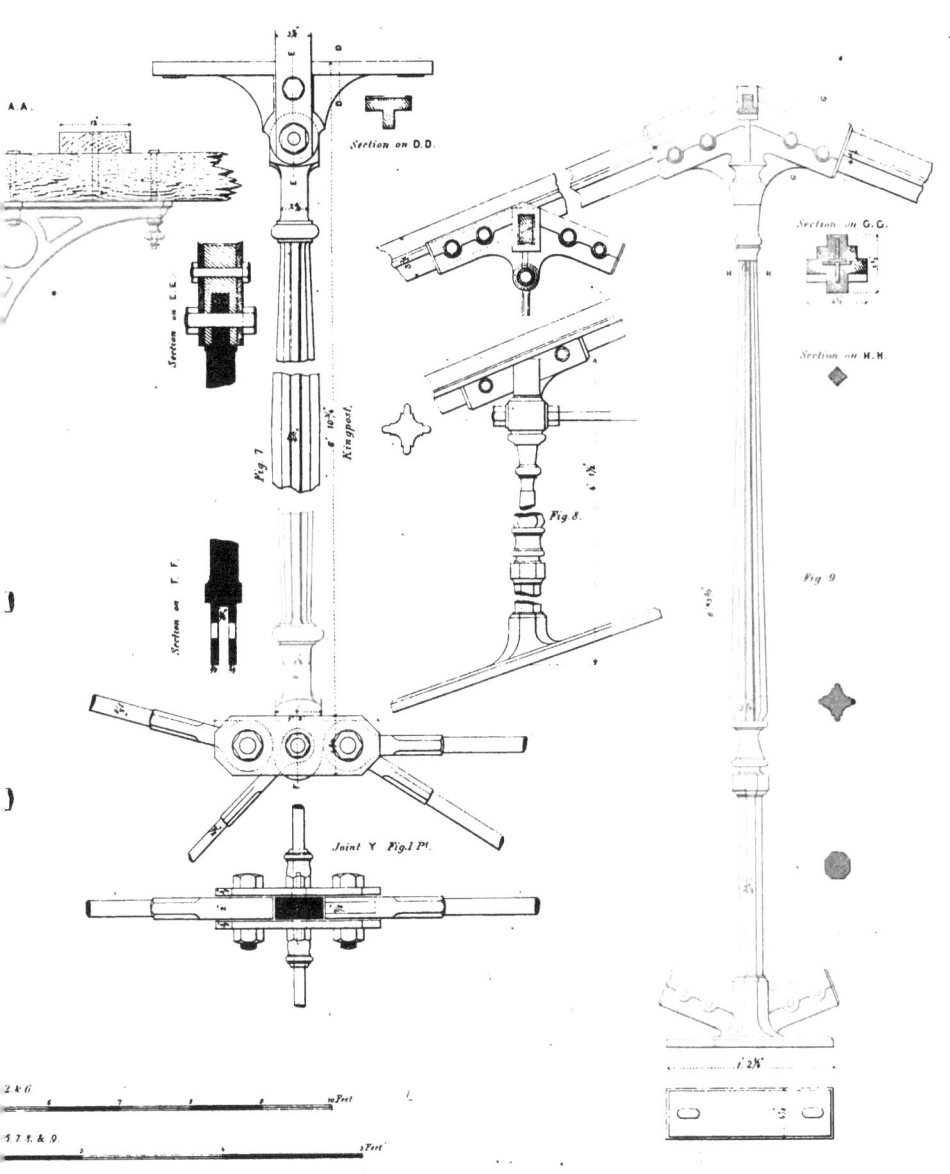

Section on D.D.

A A.

Section on E E.

Fig 7

Kingpost.

Section on F F.

Joint Y Fig.1 Pl.

Section on G.G.

Section on H.H.

Fig 8.

Fig 9

2 & 6

9, 7, 8, & 9.

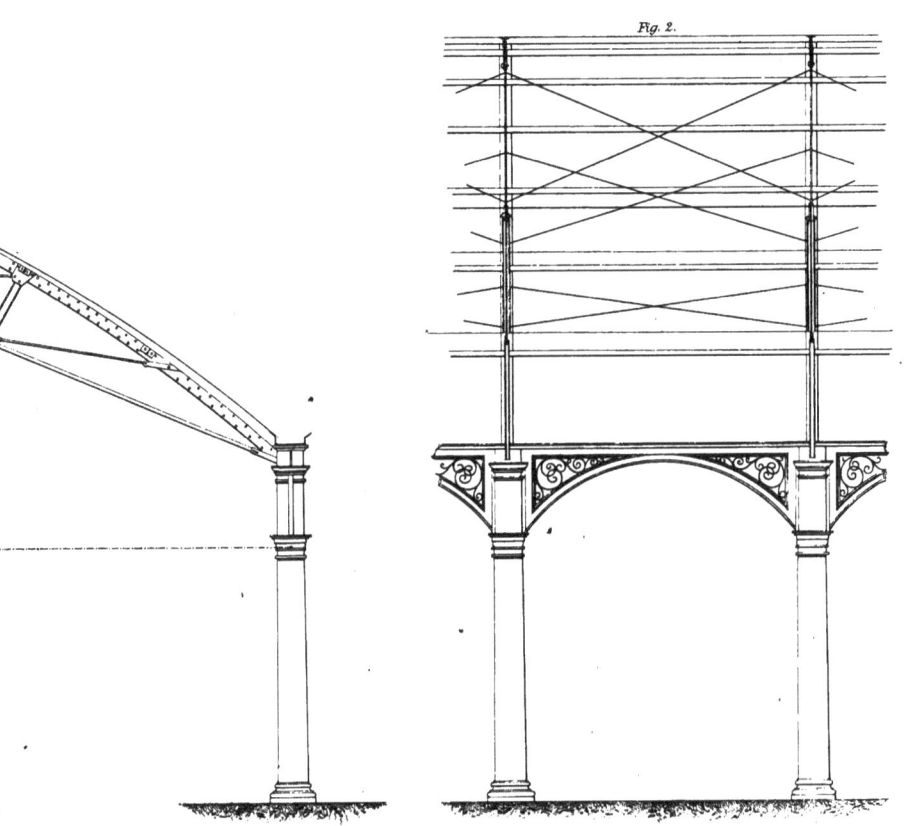

Fig. 2.

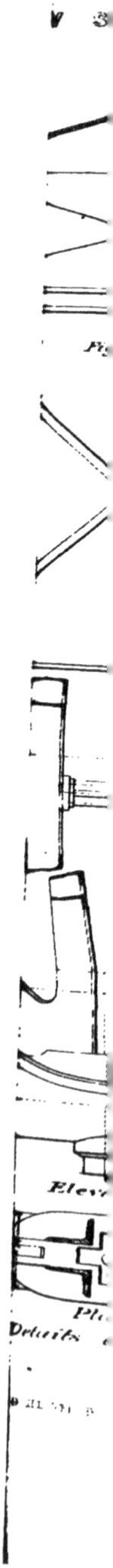

Fig

Eleva

Pl

Details

JL 3

Section on a.a

Fig. 2

Section

PLATE No. 8.

DESIGN FOR AN IRON ROOF FOR SHIP BUILDING HAVING THREE CRANES.

No. 1.

Rough Plate Glass Light.
Ventilating Louvers.
Corrugated Iron Plating.
Cast Iron Gutter.
Ventilating Sashes of Rough Plate Glass.
Rough Plate Glass Light.
Corrugated Iron Plating
Cast Iron Gutter.
73' 0"
31' 6"
80' 0"
31' 6"
Scale 10 5 0 10 20 30 40 50 Feet

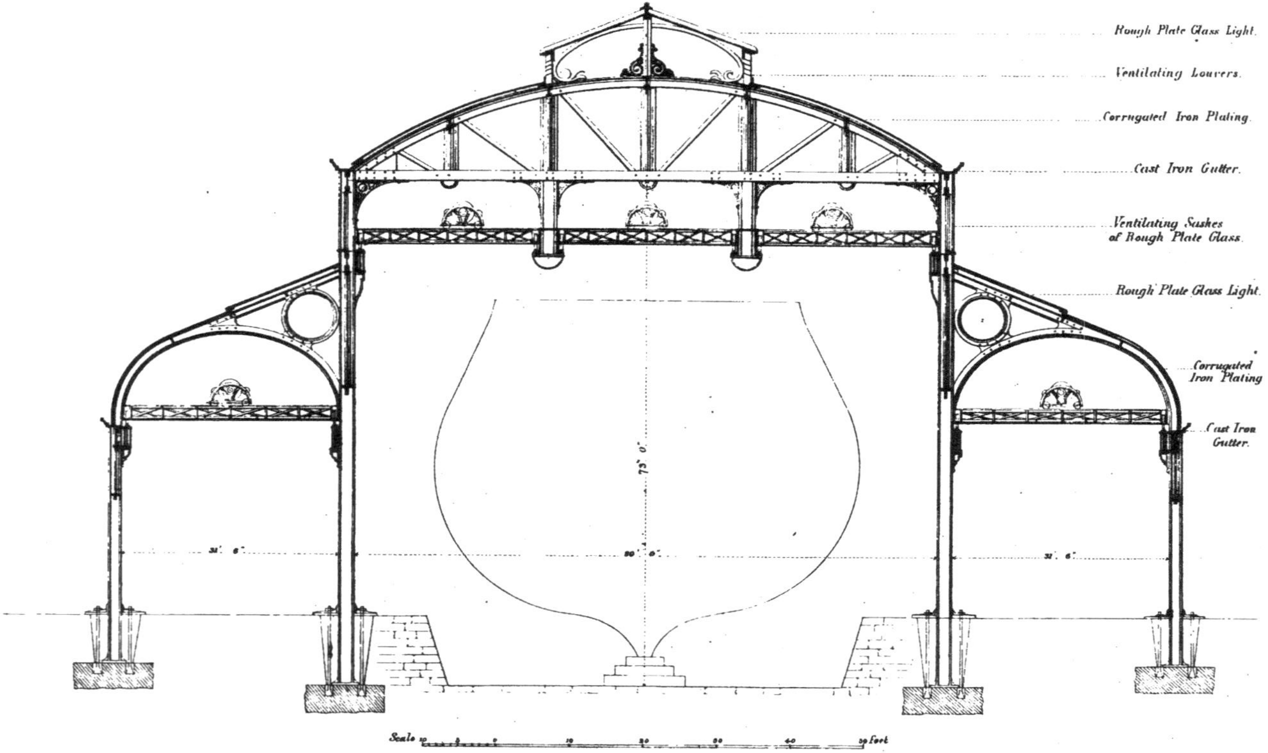

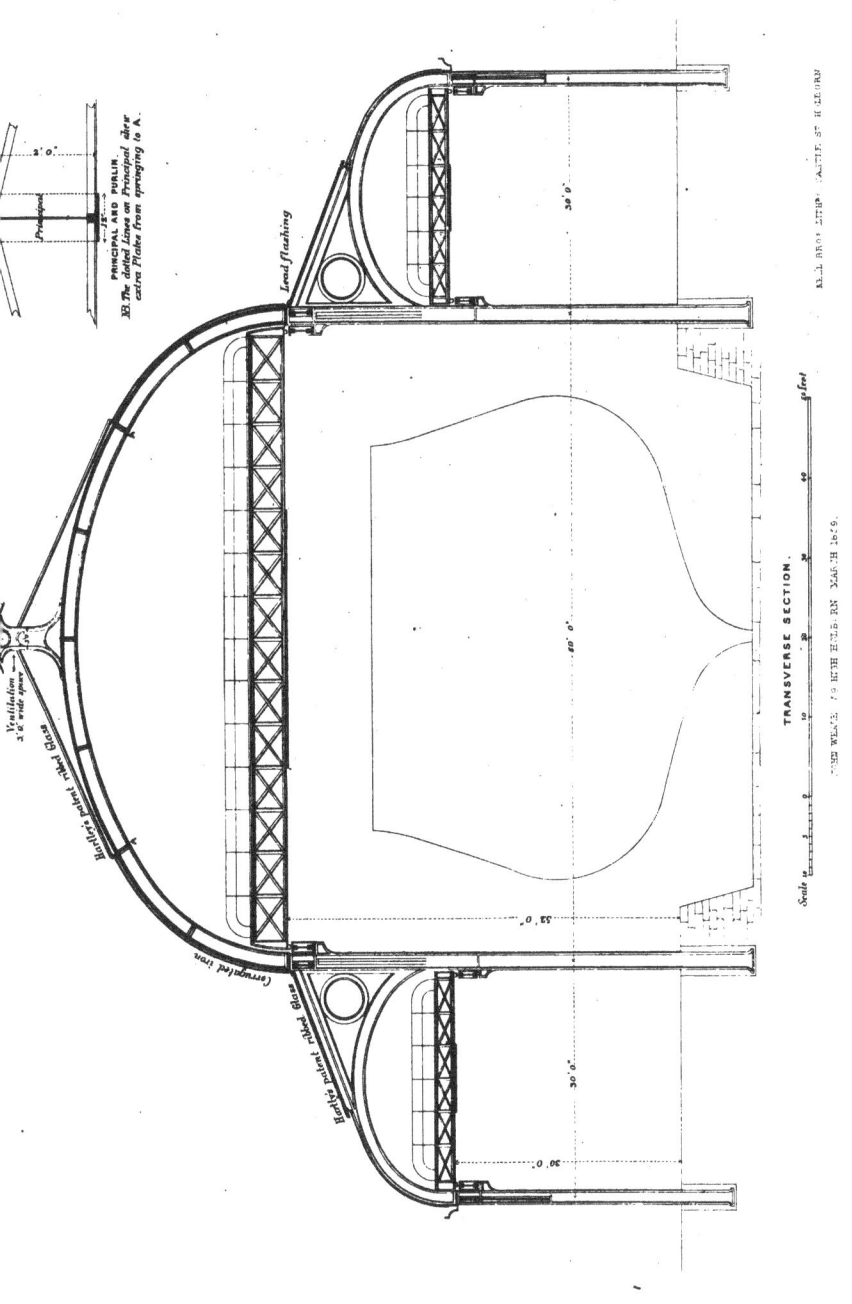

PRINCIPAL AND PURLIN.
N.B. The dotted Lines on Principal show
extra Plates from springing to A.

Principal

3' 0"

Lead flashing

Ventilation
1'6" wide space

Hartley's patent ribbed Glass

Corrugated iron

Hartley's patent ribbed Glass

33' 0"

30' 0"

30' 0"

30' 0"

30' 0"

80' 0"

TRANSVERSE SECTION.

Scale

THE WELSH HARP HOTEL, HENDON. MARCH 1879.

J.J. BROS. LITHO. CASTLE ST. HOLBORN

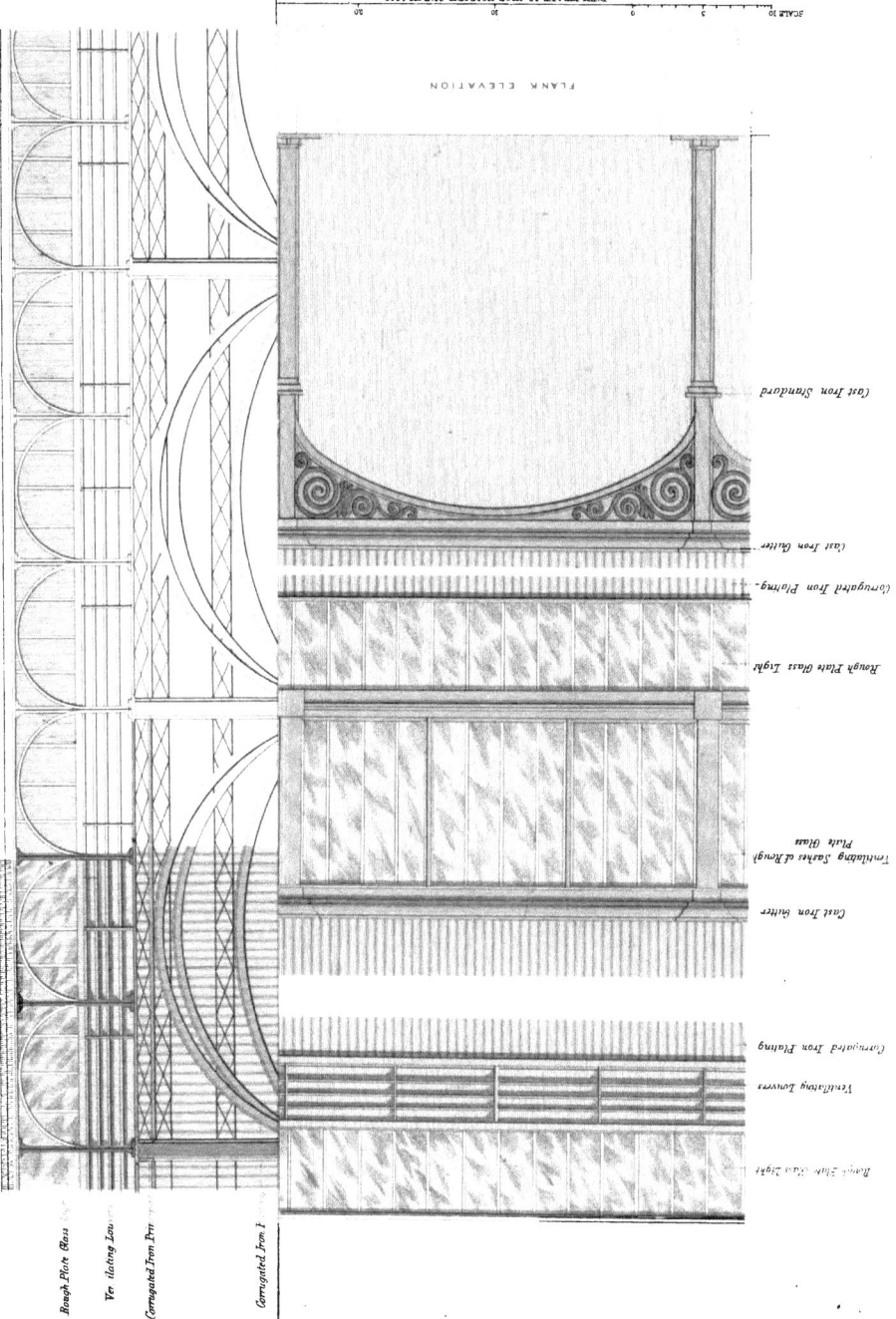

FLANK ELEVATION

SCALE 10 ... 5 0 10 20

JOHN WHALE, 59, HIGH HOLBORN, MARCH, 1859.

Cast Iron Standard

Cast Iron Gutter

Corrugated Iron Plating

Rough Plate Glass Light

Ventilating Sashes of Rough Plate Glass

Cast Iron Gutter

Corrugated Iron Plating

Ventilating Louvers

Rough Plate Glass Light

Rough Plate Glass

Ventilating Louvers

Corrugated Iron Pr...

Corrugated Iron ...

IRON ROOF FOR SHIP BUILDING.

COVERED PLAN.

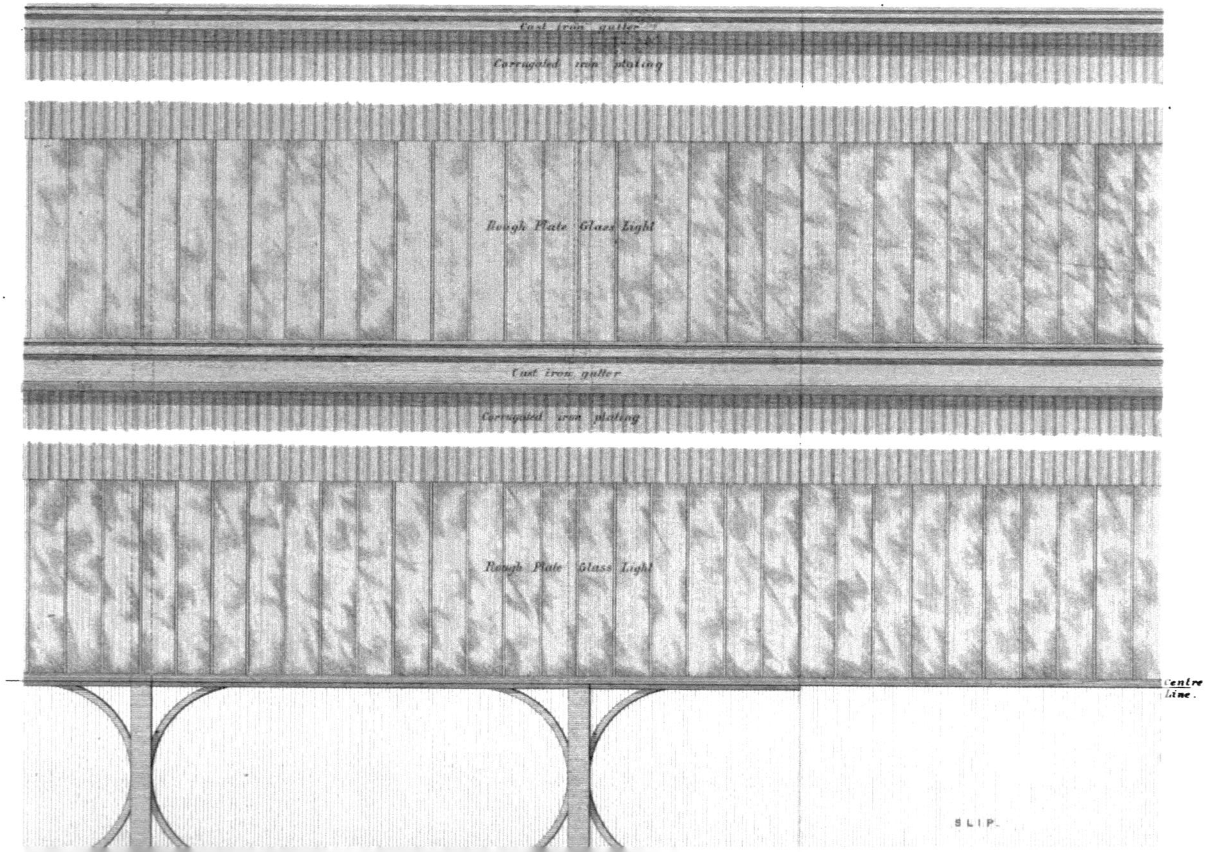

Cast iron gutter

Corrugated iron sheeting

Rough Plate Glass Light

Cast iron gutter

Corrugated iron sheeting

Rough Plate Glass Light

SLIP.

Centre line.

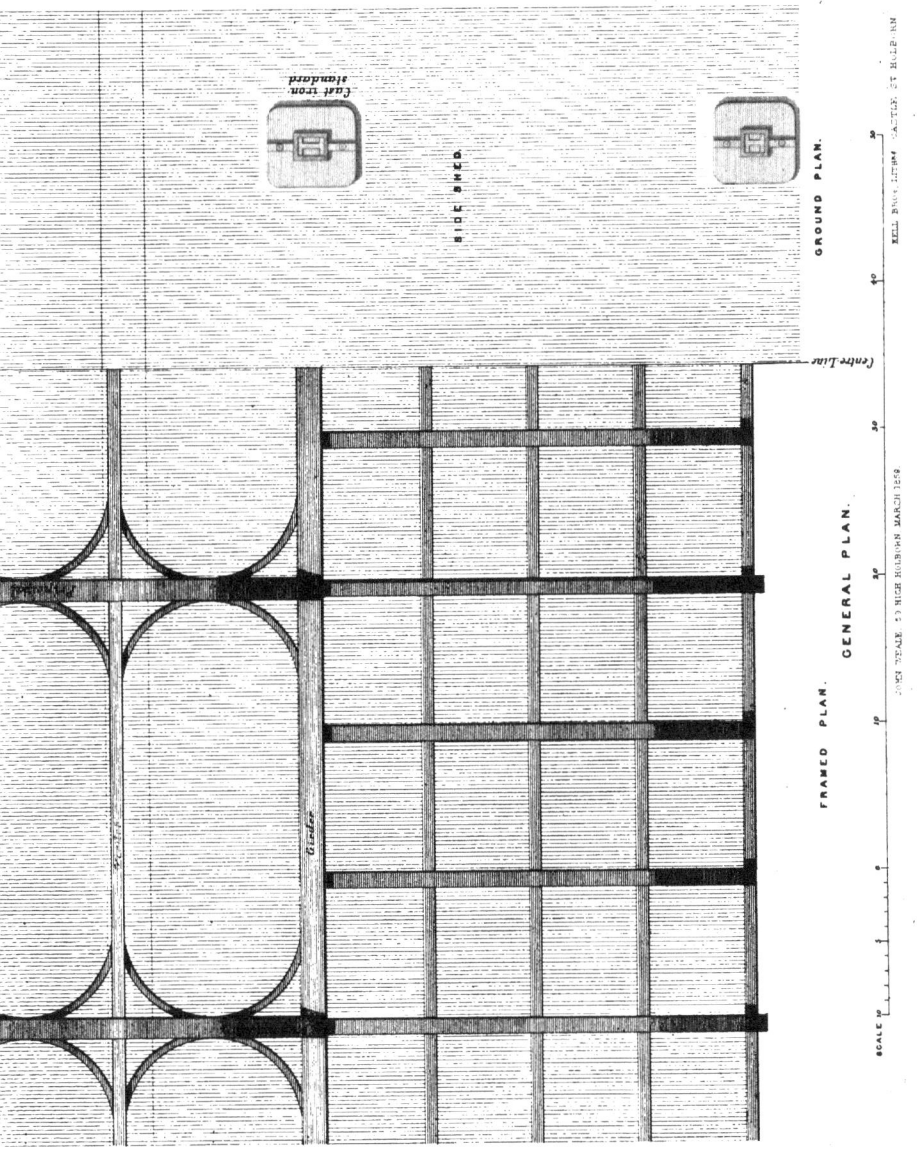

Cast iron
standard.

SIDE SHED.

GROUND PLAN.

Centre Line

Girder

FRAMED PLAN.   GENERAL PLAN.

SCALE OF

JOHN WEALE

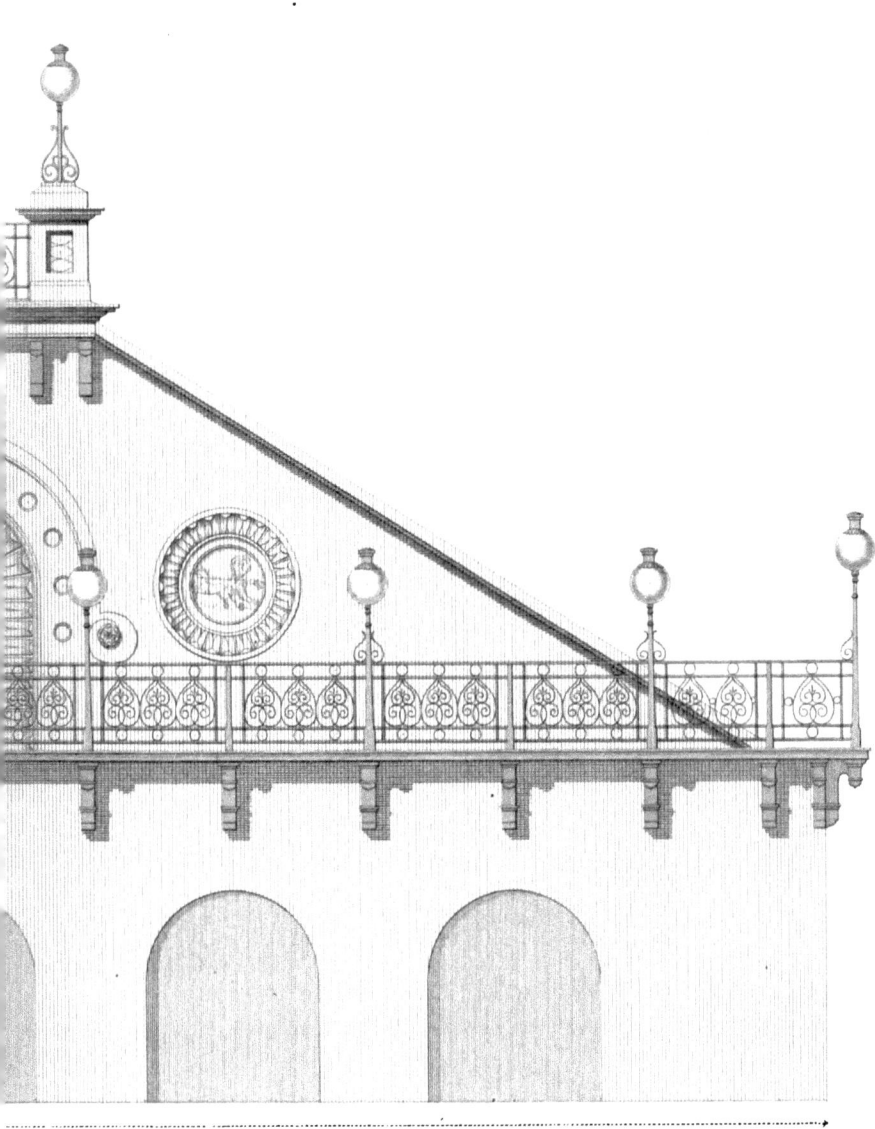

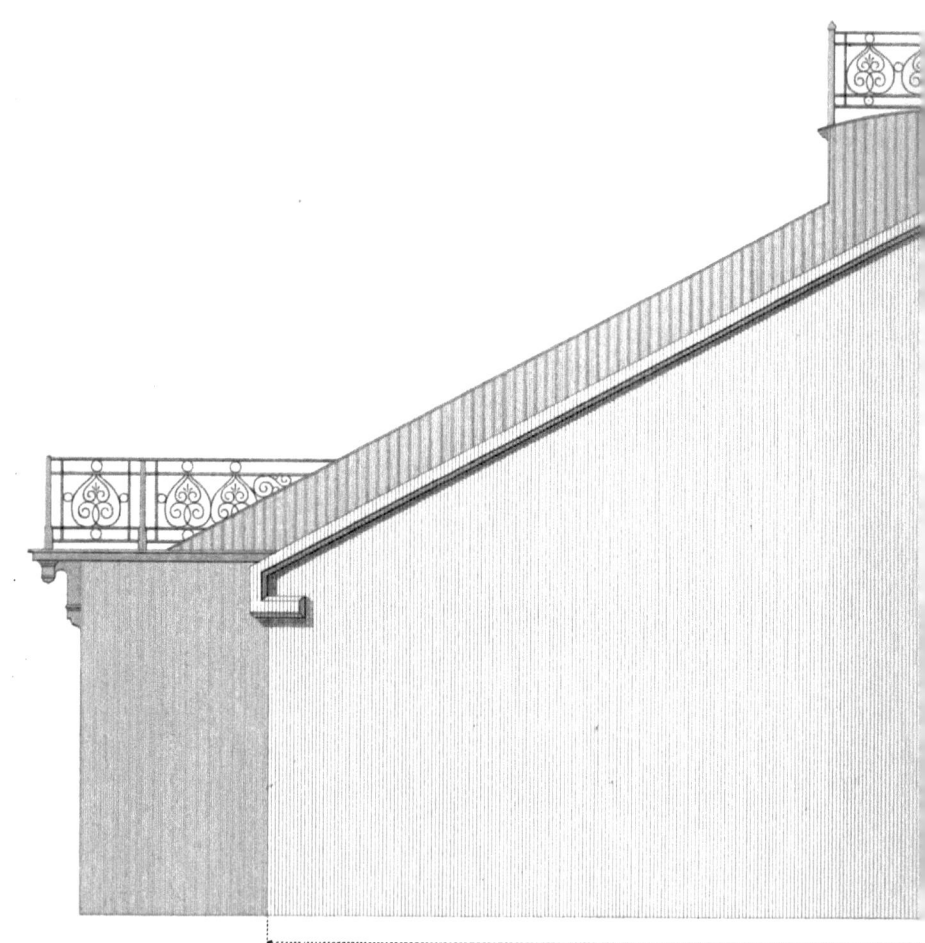

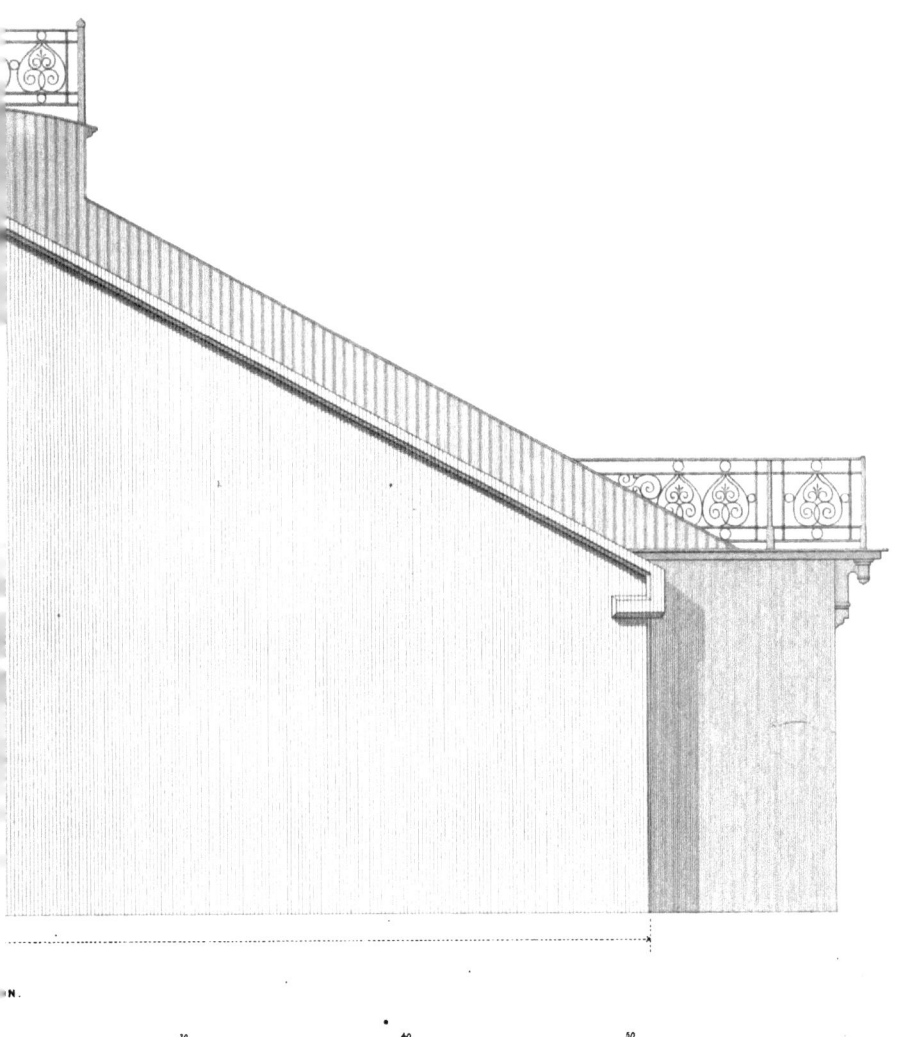

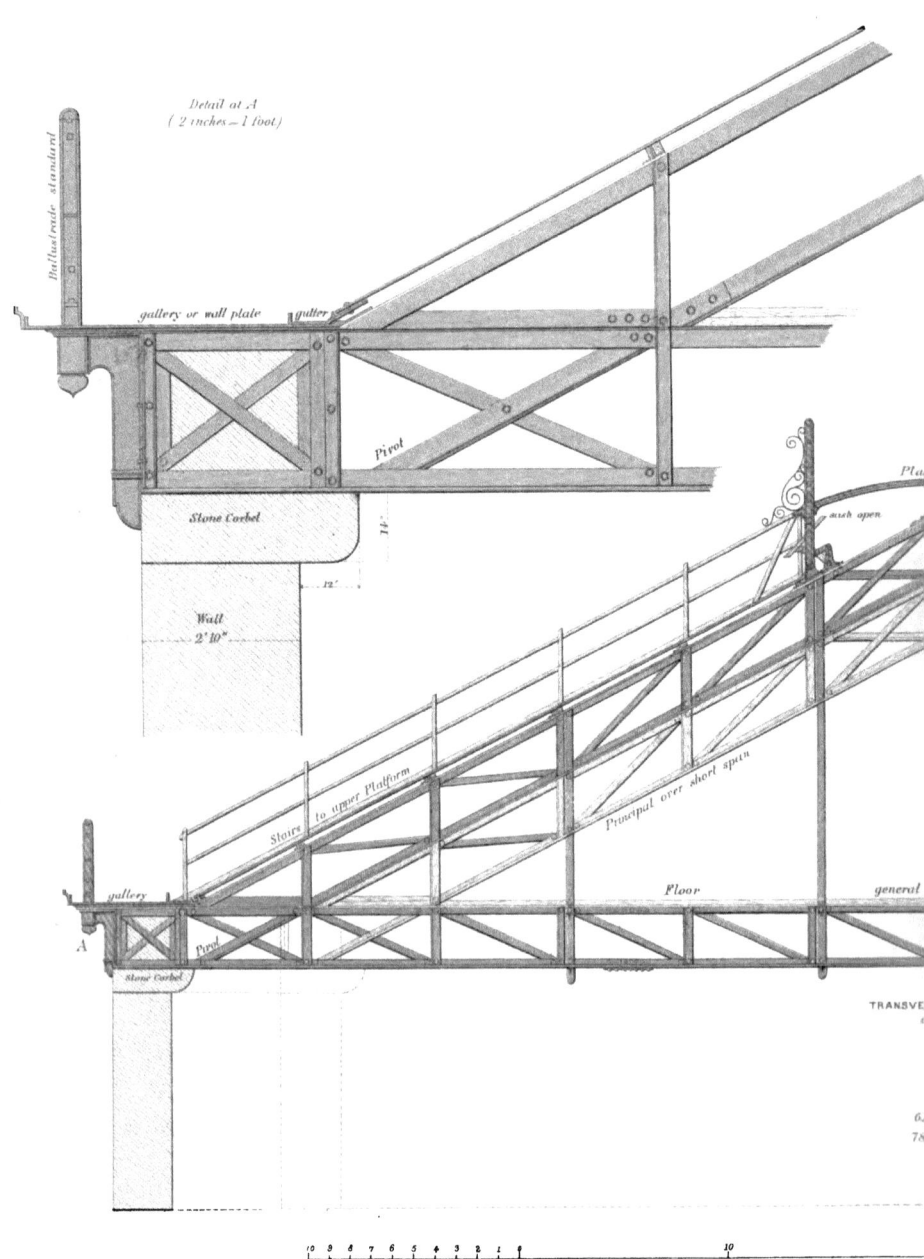

Detail at A
(2 inches = 1 foot)

Balustrade standard

gallery or wall plate

gutter

Pivot

Stone Corbel

14'

12'

Wall
2'10"

such open

Plat

Stairs to upper Platform

Principal over short span

gallery

Floor

general

Pivot

A

Stone Corbel

TRANSVE

6.

78

10 9 8 7 6 5 4 3 2 1

10

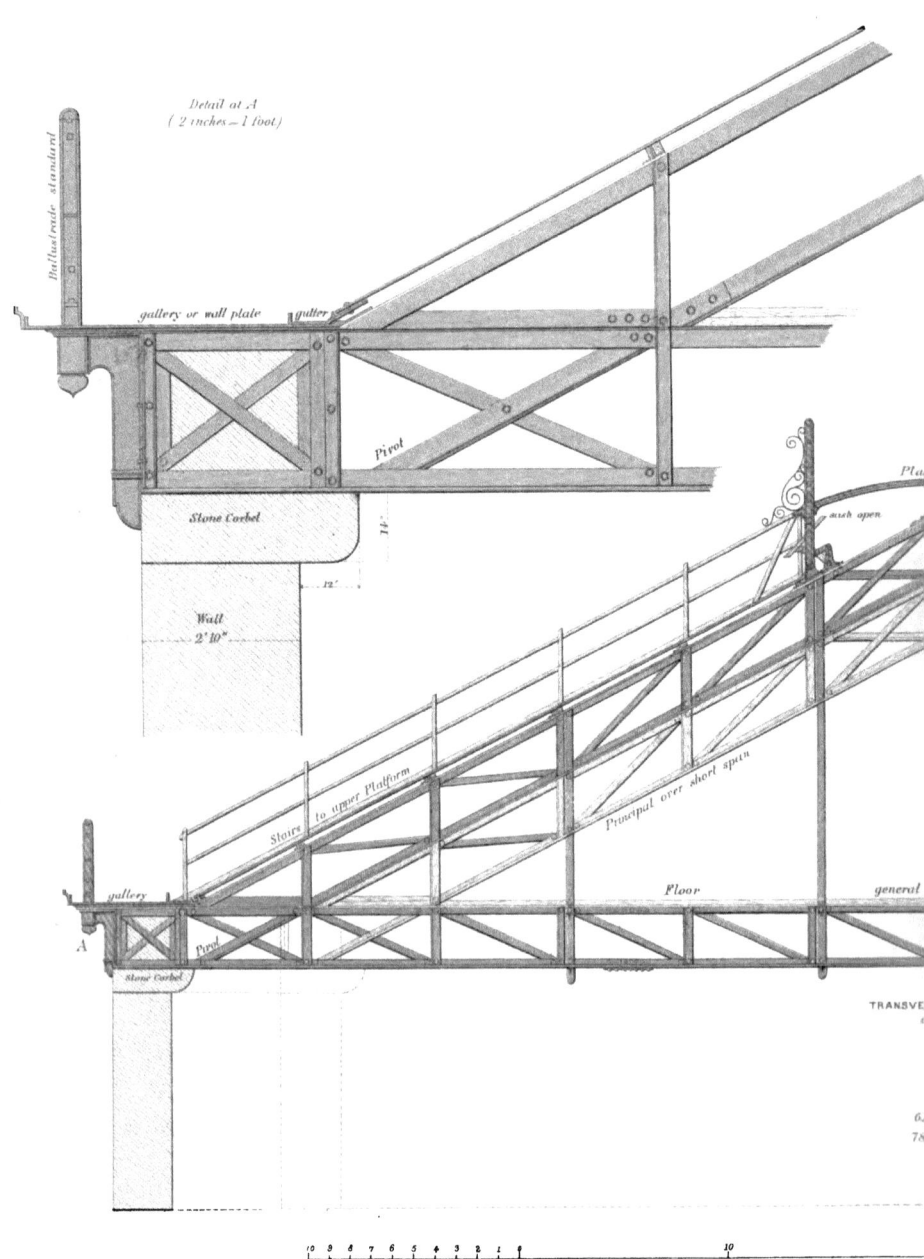

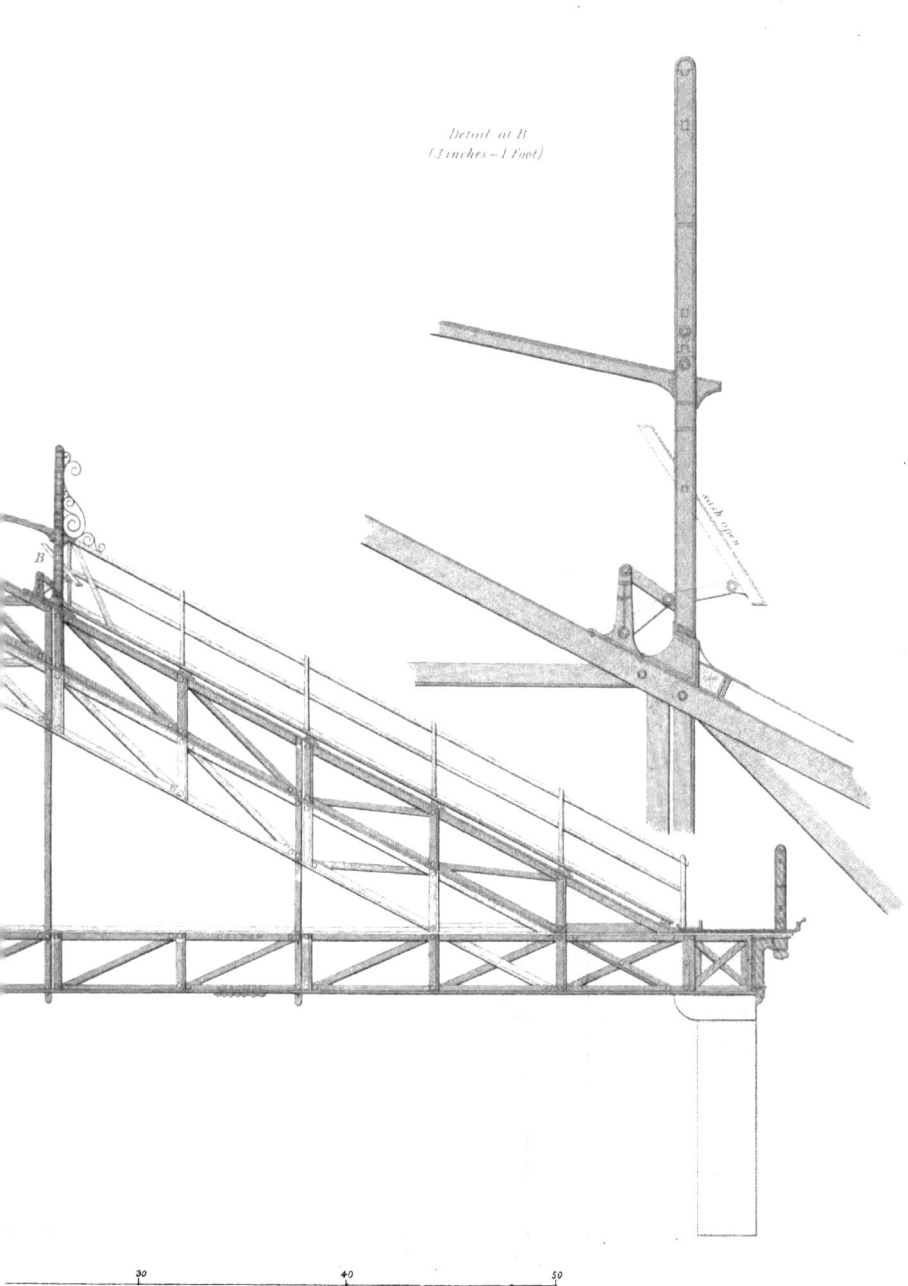

Detail at B
(3 inches = 1 foot)

B

30

40

50

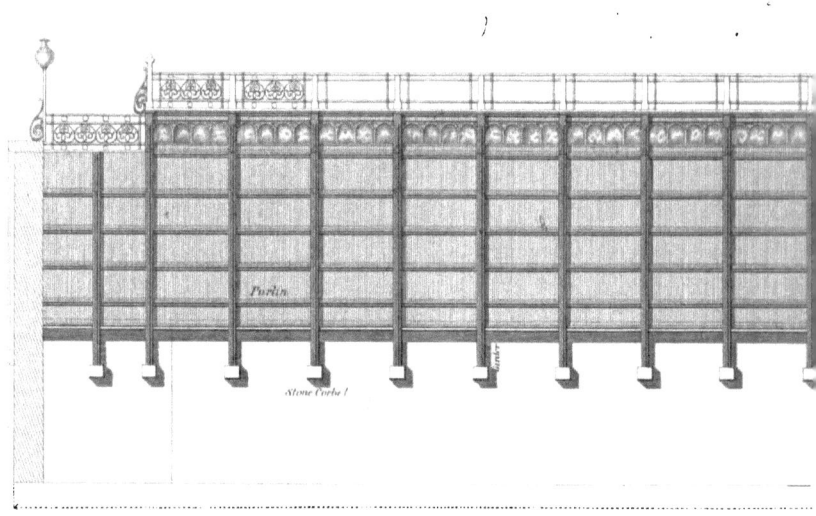

Purlin

Stone Corbel

INTERIOR

11' 4"

EXTERIO

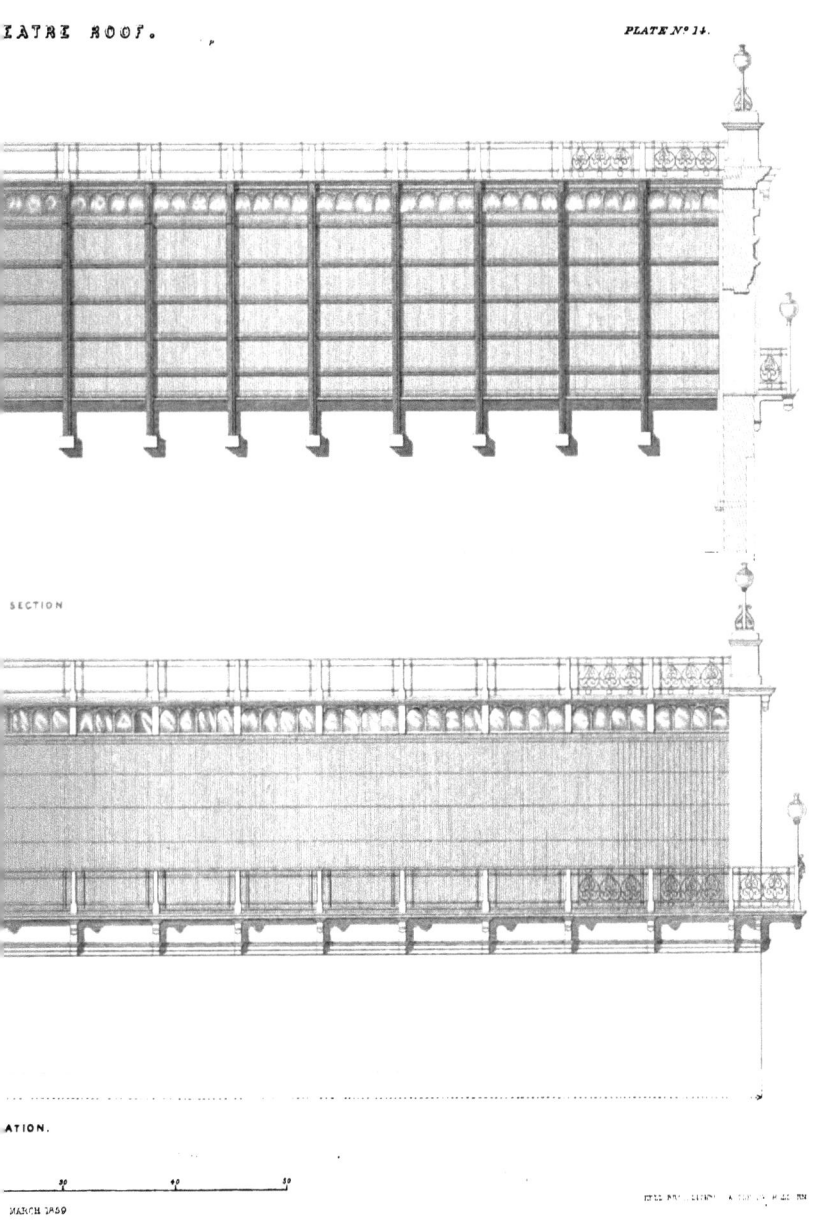

SECTION

ᴌᴀᴛɪᴏɴ.

Solid metal Plate
forming lower gallery
metal gallery

Down Pipe

Corrugated Iron Sheeting

Stone Barge over Gable

Wrought Iron Platform

14.19

11' 4"

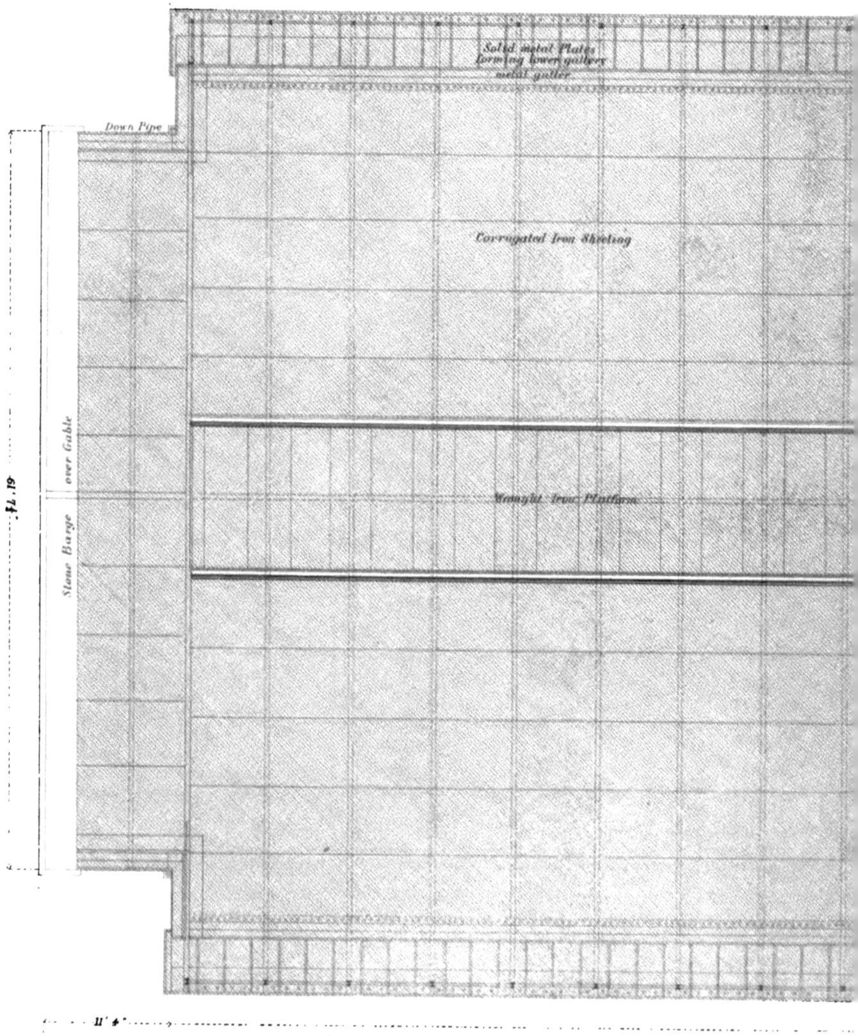

ONE HALF PLAN COVERED.

BY WYNNE

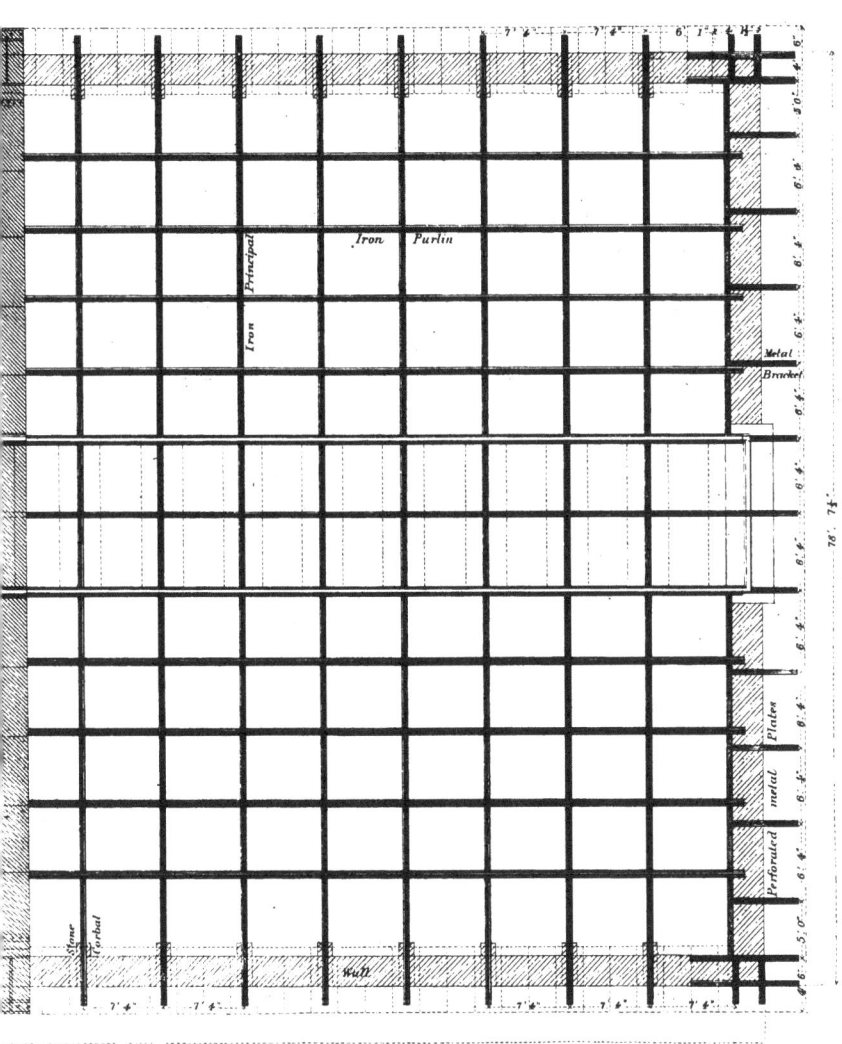

ONE HALF PLAN FRAMED.

MARCH 1859.